LITTLE IDA

THE STORY OF A FAMILY TREE

Karen Cutler Drecktrah

Little Ida
The Story of a Family Tree
Copyright © 2022 by Karen Cutler Drecktrah

This is a work of (mostly) fiction inspired by actual events, vague remembrances, comments made, and what easily can be believed happened in the lives of the Leinwander family from the mid-1930s through the early 1970s.

ISBN: 979-8-9862885-6-7
Library of Congress Control Number: 2022944787
Artwork by: Janette Labore Domke

To my husband, Bill
To my mom, Betty Leinwander Cutler, and the rest of my beloved family
To Little Ida, who reminded me where I came from

Also to:
Willard "Willie" Zapp & Glenn Schroeder
Both gone way too soon, but certainly not forgotten in
the hearts of your loved ones.

Acknowledgments

First, I'd like to thank Betty Leinwander Cutler, my mother, who originally wrote a short story about Little Ida in the 1980s as a Christmas gift to her sisters and other family members. With that story and the notes she never threw away, Little Ida was able to come to life. This story was my mother's gift, introducing me to both Grandpa (Papa George) and Grandma (Mama Ida) who both, unfortunately, passed away before I was born.

Thanks, Mom, for letting me spruce up your story!

I especially want to thank my sister and cousins, who dusted off the memory cobwebs and were able to tell me family stories I never heard before. Those instrumental were: Casey (Cutler) Korth, Jan (LaBore) Domke, Jimmy Schroeder and Shari (Schroeder) Scheibe. Jan Domke also contributed the cover and the drawings located throughout the book.

Next, I need to thank AllWriters' Workplace & Workshop, LLC, for without you, this book wouldn't be possible. Kathie Giorgio, the owner, was there every step of the way and made me realize this was possible. I also need to thank the two online workshops (the Monday Night and Thursday Night workshops) associated with AllWriters' who helped in this process, especially Carrie Newberry, who teaches the Thursday Night workshop. You all believed in Little Ida even when, at times, I had my doubts. I want you to know how much I treasure all your friendships!

I also want to thank my publisher, Deb Harris, and All Things That Matter Press who patiently waited and guided this newbie through all the steps required to publish *Little Ida.*

A huge thank you to Annette & Eric Hass, who assisted with the colorization of the sketch for the cover.

Last, but certainly not least, I thank God for putting all these pieces and people together for Little Ida and me.

MY BEGINNING

CHAPTER ONE

It took me almost all my life to realize it was odd for a tree to have a name, but I have one—I'm Little Ida. Currently, I'm by myself and quite tired. But it *is* giving me some time to reflect about my life and wonderful family.

Before I tell my tale, there's one thing that it's important to know about us spruce trees: we carry generations of knowledge in our roots. We've observed people for centuries, learned their ways, and carry this knowledge with us throughout our generations. I think, if someone could somehow put a cross section of our trunks on a record player, the rings would not only tell our age, but also play the songs of our knowledge, heart, and spirit.

***

My story began on a farm during the Depression in the middle of the 1930s. It was a normal farm, for the most part. Besides animals and vegetables, the farmer also grew spruce trees. I'm proud to say I am a blue spruce, a most promising and very sought-after tree, although at the time, I certainly didn't look the part. All my other siblings looked better; they were a bit taller, their branches were full of needles, and they had beautiful, conical shapes. I was scrawny, my branches weren't as long as theirs and didn't have quite as many needles on those branches to give me that same full shape. However, I knew all I needed was some love and I'd be something special.

The day I found my forever home is one I remember well. It started out as an ordinary, warm August morning. There was a gentle breeze and I could smell the dampness emanating from the grass.

I woke up at dawn and gazed around at my brothers and sisters. I'd never met my parents. They were long gone before I even grew out of the ground. We were planted on a small hill, overlooking the farm buildings. It was a beautiful place and I loved having all my siblings around me.

There were different groups of us trees, all at various stages of growth. Even though our group was only about three feet tall, we were the tallest and, being seven years old, currently the oldest group. I was proud of us, because we were the lucky ones that had lived this long. Half of my brothers and sisters died along the way, most to a disease, a few to a bad hailstorm at the beginning of summer, and three to some boys who pulled them up by the roots for some unknown reason. Boy, was the farmer mad when he found out about it.

About an hour after I woke up, I saw the farmer coming up the hill, pushing his wheelbarrow. Every day prior to today, it was always full of soil and mulch that he put all around the ground where our roots were. This time, though, the wheelbarrow was empty, except for the shovel he used to spread around the dirt.

I wondered what was going on. It looked like I'd find out soon; he was heading right for us with the shovel in his hand.

He started at the opposite end from where I was. Standing in front of one of my siblings, he took a deep breath and plunged the shovel into the ground.

What is he doing? It looks like he's digging her out.

He worked the shovel in a circle around her, then slowly pulled her out and laid her gently on her side. He went back to the wheelbarrow and brought out a piece of burlap that had been hidden at the bottom. He returned, picked her up, and proceeded to set her roots in the middle of the burlap sack piece. Then he cautiously pulled it up from the corners and tied the cloth together just under her bottom branches with some rope. He then lowered her into the wheelbarrow.

She looks fine, all snuggled in the burlap wrapped around her roots. Oh, he's coming back. I know what's going on. I've seen this happening the last couple of years. He took those other groups away, but I don't know where they went. Since he takes such good care of us, it must be someplace wonderful.

The farmer then went to the next sibling in line and repeated the procedure, keeping at it until the wheelbarrow was full. He turned the wheelbarrow around and started down the hill. About fifteen minutes later, he came back. Once again, he dug up more of my brothers and sisters, wrapped their roots, and put them in the wheelbarrow.

Until I was the only one left.

While he was loading my last sibling in the wheelbarrow, I thought, *I'm scared. I don't know which is worse, being dug up and taken away or being left behind. Wait, he never left any of the other trees behind. What if he decides I'm not worthy of anything and throws me away? I'm not quite as tall as my brothers and sisters and I'm skinny and ugly compared to them.*

The farmer came back and interrupted my thoughts. I straightened out my branches to look more filled out. He hovered over me, leaning on the handle of the shovel. "What should I do with you?" the farmer said out loud. "You're still sorta the runt, but you're looking a bit better than you did a couple of weeks ago when I last checked you. I can't let you stay here, because I need the space to start a new batch of saplings."

I used every ounce of strength to straighten my branches even more and reach as high as I could toward the sky. *Please take me with you.*

Please!

He paused silently for another minute, then started to shovel around me, just like the others. He used the shovel to lift me out of the ground and onto the remaining burlap that was laid out on the ground. I thought it would hurt, being ripped out of the ground, but the farmer was so gentle I didn't feel a thing. He pulled up the corners of the burlap, tucked them under my branches, and used some rope to tie everything together. He placed me in a tiny space that was left in the wheelbarrow and went down the hill.

When we got to the barn, I saw the first bunch of my siblings lined up in the back of his pickup truck. He put the rest of us in there, too. Then the farmer loaded crates that contained a variety of vegetables and drove away from the farm. I wasn't sure where I was headed, but I was excited to be going.

CHAPTER TWO

The ride was extremely bumpy and I was saved from tipping over twice only because we were packed in tightly together. All I was able to see was the blue sky above, since the sides of the truck were too high for me.

An hour or so later, he drove into a parking lot behind a store, where several trucks and tents were scattered about. The farmer set up a table, then he unpacked all the vegetables and put them on it. Once he'd done that, he took us off the truck, two by two, and lined all us saplings on the ground in front of the table—to show us off, I figured. After he took care of us, he headed back into the cab of his truck and brought back sheets of paper which I noticed contained prices.

He is going to sell us.

There was a lot of noise. Pigs were oinking, hens were clucking and a lot of children were running around, laughing and screaming. *I sure hope I don't have to be here all day. I'm not used to this noise. Our field was really quiet.*

It didn't take long for the farmer's first customer to come along. "I see you have a new crop of spruce trees ready to go, just like you promised."

"Yep. Depending on the size, the prices range from two dollars to five."

"Hmm, let me have a look-see. How much are you selling that one for?" he asked, pointing at me. "Hope you're giving it away, 'cause it isn't going to be worth your time," he added, laughing.

All my efforts to keep my scrawny limbs up to impress people blew away, just like the cold wind last December. My entire trunk sagged with the hopelessness of my situation.

"Oh, it's a little on the tiny and thin side, but I think with the right type of soil, it'll come around. It was the last one planted and didn't quite get the sunlight the others did," the farmer replied as he walked around the table to help the rude customer.

"I'm sure you will be selling that tale all day, instead of that tree. I'll take a four dollar one."

Encouraged by what the farmer said, I tried to straighten up and look the best I could.

The farmer came to the front of the table and pointed to two of my siblings. "These two are that price. Pick whichever one you want."

The man picked one of my brothers, paid the farmer, and took off. *I was glad he was gone.*

As the day went on and the rest of my brothers and sisters were sold, I wondered if I was ever going to find a home. Between the desperation of my situation and the August heat attacking me from above and the heat radiating from the pavement below, it was getting harder and harder to be at my best. I started to droop. I saw the farmer begin to gather the remaining vegetables, but he stopped when a young man sauntered over.

"Looks like you've sold almost all your stuff," the man said.

"Yep, just a few vegetables and, oh, the tiny tree in front. Nobody's even looked at that one, so I'll probably toss it when I get home. It's a shame, really. It didn't get much sunlight where it was planted."

Toss me? You mean throw me out? No!

Suddenly, a shadow fell over me, and, as I looked up, I saw a friendly, gray-haired lady walking toward me. *This is* it. *She's the one. She'll give me a home. She must."*

I mustered up the strength to once again stretch out my tiny limbs and straighten my trunk the best I could, so she would notice me.

She bent down, looked at me and said, "What a nice little tree." She looked up at the farmer and asked, "How much?"

He said, "Well, that's going to be a very good tree, so she's a real bargain at two dollars."

She turned toward the young man. "What do you think about this tree, Kelly?"

He walked around to the front of the table, knelt down, and looked me over. He then got up and said to the farmer, "Well, it's getting late in the day. Instead of hauling the tree back to your farm to throw it out, maybe we can make a deal?"

The farmer sighed, looked at both the young man and older lady, and shook his head. "Okay, here's what I'll do. I'll sell you the little tree for a dollar-fifty."

Please have enough money. Please take me home with you. Don't let me get thrown out!

The lady dug in her big black purse and pulled out some coins. With some reluctance, she started counting. Fifty cents, one dollar, a dollar twenty-five, a dollar forty-five, up to a dollar forty-six. She scraped the bottom of her purse, found a few more coins, and counted out forty-seven, forty-eight, forty-nine, and, as her head looked up to the sky, she jammed her hand into the depths of that purse. "Oh, I think there's a hole in the lining ... right ... about ... here. Maybe, just maybe ...." She scrabbled around more in her purse, her tongue poking out while she searched. "Aha!" She then successfully pulled out the very last penny. "Here's your one-fifty." When she bent down to pick me up, her nose twitched and I saw a twinkle in her eye. My needles tingled as she carried me to the car.

She gently cradled me in her arms, only relinquishing me to the young man for a couple of moments while she got settled in the front seat. Her arms stretched toward me and, once she had me back in her hands, she placed me on her lap for the ride to my new home.

I tried very hard to tuck my sharp needles toward me so I didn't hurt her. I might not have had many of them, but since she was taking such good care of me, the least I could do was keep my needles away from her face. The ride in the car was much smoother than in the back of the pickup. And, since I was sitting on the lady's lap, I could see out the window. First, we drove past a lot of tall buildings that were together, then we drove over a long bridge that crossed a rapidly moving river. After the car rolled up a steep hill, we pulled up in front of a huge, two-story cream-and-green-colored house located on the corner of two streets. There were steps leading to a small porch, covered by a roof. *The door on the other side of the porch must lead into her house*, I thought. Planted flowers trimmed the base of the porch and the house.

Two girls sat on the steps, talking with a man sitting on one of the chairs on the porch. He looked to be about the same age as my new owner. The gray-haired lady carefully got out of the car, proudly walked up to them and announced, "Look at this little spruce tree I found at the pig fair. I'm going to plant her in the back, next to the house, where the roses used to be."

The man turned toward her. "I thought you were getting more flowers to plant there. Why a tree?"

"I wanted something that would last long after I'm gone, something I could be remembered by."

The man chuckled. "Ida, I believe you are already unforgettable, but we'll help you plant Little Ida tomorrow, wherever you want her to go."

The lady smiled brightly. "Little Ida. That's genius, George!"

From then on, I had a name. I was Little Ida. I was the luckiest tree that ever sprouted!

CHAPTER THREE

For safekeeping, they placed me on the porch, next to the stairs leading into the house, for the night. The porch faced west, so while the sun was setting, I wondered about my new family, where exactly my new home would be on the property, and my good fortune that the lady liked me enough to buy me. Then I thought about my siblings, hoping they'd found as happy a home as I seemed to. I finally dozed off until noise coming from inside the house woke me up the next morning.

My new family is going to plant me today.

Eventually, everyone came out of the house. The lady picked me up and showed me off to those family members who weren't there yesterday. I counted eight people—no, wait, there was a ninth one, a little boy about two years old, being held by the younger man that helped buy me.

Nine people live in that house? Oh, boy.

After they oohed and ahhed at me for a couple minutes, the group followed Ida down a narrow sidewalk that went to the east side of the house. Kelly put the boy down, saying, "Why don't you play in your sandbox, Jimmy?" Then the two men got shovels and began to dig a hole large enough to put me in.

"Are you sure this isn't too close to the house? The tree's going to grow, you know," Kelly said to George.

"No, Kelly," George replied. "I think it'll be fine here. It will give this side of the house more shade in the summer. Besides, I don't think this tree will grow as large as others like it. Didn't you say last night the farmer told you it was the smallest one of the bunch?"

"I think it still will grow pretty tall, even if she was the smallest. The farmer also told me it initially was in a spot that didn't get as much sun as the others. I think once we start taking care of it, this tree will certainly be big."

"Well, I'd prefer it closer to the house to protect it from the weather coming in from the west while it's growing. Don't you think that's a good idea?" Ida interjected.

I want to be close to the house, too.

Kelly sighed. "Okay, okay. Two against one. Right here is where Little Ida is going."

Once the hole was finished, Ida gave me to Kelly and he set me gently into it. Then both men used their shovels to fill the dirt back in around me, while adding some extra smelly dirt with it.

Jimmy, the little boy, raced over to the group of adults while Kelly was using a hose to water the fresh ground. "Eeeww. Bad smell!"

Kelly smiled. "It's called manure. It's supposed to smell bad, but it will help Little Ida grow."

"It smells like poopie."

"That's because it is. It's cow poopie."

"Cow poopie, cow poopie," the little boy kept shouting and running around, while the youngest-looking girl chased after him.

"Now look what you started, Kelly. How am I going to stop him from saying that?" the tallest and oldest-looking of the girls said to the young man.

"Don't worry, Lucy. He'll forget about it by supper," Kelly said with a smile.

After they planted me in the ground, most of them went back in the house, but a couple of the girls stayed outside and played catch. Me? After all the excitement of being planted and now snuggled in the ground with nutritious food, water and with the August sun beaming down on me, I fell asleep.

I woke up after the sun set. The windows in the house were open and I heard various noises that I would eventually come to know by heart. Since I was close to the house and windows, I couldn't wait until I got tall enough to see in. I'd just have to be patient.

One more voice was heard loud and clear after the house quieted down for the night.

"Cow poopie!"

I'm going to love my new home.

CHAPTER FOUR

My new family had a great big yard, even though they lived in the city. They had large vegetable and flower gardens, a couple apple trees, some bushes with berries growing on them, a rhubarb patch, and a few chickens in the back for eggs—and the occasional dinner.

The perfume of the flower gardens and budding fruit trees during the spring and early summer brought me the joy of a fresh new year. Late summer and early fall emitted aromas of canning their bounty; the sour smells of pickling cucumbers and beets and the scent of canning berries and apples, including the making of applesauce. During late fall, the smell turned musty from leftover apples and dying leaves being burned that warned me that winter approached.

Besides the house, there was a smaller structure they used to store the car and all the gardening tools. Scattered around the yard were birdbaths and four different types of birdhouses. Lots of birds, rabbits, and squirrels also called the huge yard home, and, over the years, I got to know several of them. When I got strong enough, some of the birds and squirrels even built nests in my branches.

My owner's name was Ida Leinwander. Mama Ida, as I began to call her. Mama Ida was a stout German woman who had long, gray hair she carefully tied into a bun daily. Even though she was older, her blue eyes shone bright and loving. She loved being outside whenever she could. On nice days, she even brought some of her chores out with her.

She was married to Papa George. He was the man who'd named me. He also was of German heritage, stood about the same height as Mama Ida, and hair that was graying at the temples. I overheard that he worked in a mill down by the river. He worked a lot of hours, as a foreman, to support his large family, so he wasn't around very much. When he was, however, he loved to putter in the yard, do woodworking—especially making duck decoys—or just relax by smoking his rolled-up cigarettes and reading the newspaper. He didn't say much, but it was hard to get a word in edgewise with the large family. He also loved to hunt and fish and usually brought home a lot of game to help feed them all.

They were the proud parents of five daughters, in order: Lucille, Bernice, Gerrie, Pearl, and Betty. All were beautiful, athletic, and smart, but I soon learned they each had their own personality.

***

Soon after I was planted, Mama Ida and Papa George were walking outside near me when Mama Ida suddenly stopped and turned to him. "George, do you think you can take a short break from making duck decoys in your woodshop and make me a small bench to put next to Little Ida? I'm thinking I might want to sit out here by her while I do some of my chores. You tell me I need to get outside more. Would you be able to do that?"

Papa George looked at the space a moment, then replied, "I should be able to. I haven't made anything furniture-related in a while, but Kelly should be able to help me. I'm guessing besides a seat, you'd like a back on it also."

"Ah, George. You know me too well. Maybe you can make it long enough for both of us to sit on. A place where you can enjoy the newspaper on a nice day."

"I'm not the only one who knows their spouse well," Papa George said with a chuckle.

"How long do you think it will take? Will you be able to get it done before late fall so we can enjoy it this year? Don't worry about the varnish or paint. I'll take care of that part once you're done. But please make sure it's sanded. I don't want you to have to dig splinters out of my behind."

After they both laughed, Papa George thought for a moment. "I do have varnish and, if you don't mind white, I have a pail left over from when I repainted the boat this spring."

"That should work. Maybe Bernie might like to paint some flowers on it when she's back next summer. I know how much she loves the arts and crafts classes she's taking at college. Next time I write her, I'll mention it." Then Mama Ida took Papa George by the hand and continued their walk.

How wonderful. Mama Ida and even Papa George will be able to spend more time with me.

***

A couple weeks later, Papa George proudly carried out a small bench, complete with back and arms on each side. He set it in the middle of the yard and yelled, "Ida, come out here. Your bench is ready."

Soon, I heard a door slam and she came out, wiping her hands on her apron. "Oh, George, that looks beautiful." Then she reached down and ran the palm of her hand against both the seat and the back of it. "Smooth, too. Nice job. I can work on varnishing tomorrow and, with the weather still being warm, it should dry enough so I can paint it on Tuesday. It's not supposed to rain in the next few days, is it?"

"I already checked the Farmer's Almanac. No rain for a week," Papa George answered with a slight smirk on his face.

It's already pretty. I can't wait for it to get all painted up.

During the rest of the summer and into early fall, every time Papa George watered the garden, he always gave me an extra squirt or put special mulch around my roots. He'd say, "My Ida would get awfully mad at me if something happened to you, Little Ida, so I need to take extra special care of you." Then he'd give me a wink that I'd noticed he only gave to people he cared about.

***

It didn't take me long to sort out the rest of the family, either.

Lucille, or Lucy as the family called her, the eldest, was grown and married to Kelly, the young man who'd helped Mama Ida buy me. Both she and Kelly loved to garden, Kelly more so. They lived in an upstairs apartment in the house, so she helped Mama Ida while Kelly worked. Mama Ida loved it because her grandson, Jimmy, was around for her to love and spoil. Lucy had just found out she was pregnant with her second child not long after I was planted.

Bernice, or Bernie, the second oldest, was close to finishing college in Oshkosh, the first and only daughter to go. She was studying to be a grade school teacher. Most of the year, she was gone, but she always came home during the summers and holidays to help around the house and play ball with her sisters. Mama Ida and Papa George were proud of her, but hated that she lived away from home most of the year.

Right before Bernie headed back to school that first year, she curled up on my bench, reading a book. Papa George strolled out and stopped in front of her. She looked up and sat upright, making space for him to sit down.

He looked at her and asked, "Why do you want to be a teacher so much? You're so smart, you could be anything you want."

"Well, Dad, I love kids and hope to have my own someday, but until then, I want to teach children how to read, so no matter what's happening in their lives, they can go to the library, pick out a book, and travel to wherever they want, even if it's only for a while. That's how I feel. It's kind of hard to explain."

Papa George got up from the bench and looked at Bernie with admiration in his eyes. "No, I believe you've explained it to me exactly right. You will make a fantastic teacher."

Her face turned a slight shade of pink and she smiled with delight. "Thanks, Dad," she replied, hugging him.

Geraldine, or Gerrie, the middle girl, had graduated high school a couple months before I arrived. She was thin, smart, energetic, and very competitive. No matter where Gerrie was going, to the park to play ball, to her friends' homes, or just doing her chores outside, she *never* just walked anywhere. She seemed to always scurry around from one thing to another. She was looking for a job, and, every morning, she set out on foot, headed towards town to "pound the pavement," as she put it whenever she was around. She always returned early in the afternoon to help Mama Ida around the house.

One day, she was in the garden with Mama Ida cutting rhubarb. "No offense, Mom, but I really don't like doing all this housework. I want to work, but I'm beginning to worry that I'll never land a job."

"Well, remember, times are still tough around here and a lot of places aren't hiring. Don't fret, you'll find a job soon enough. And believe me, as much as I like having the help, you're too fidgety for me. But you will need to know how to do most of these things when you get married."

"Married? Me? I'm not planning on getting married. I doubt any guy will put up with me."

Mama Ida shook her head. "We'll see, Gerrie. We'll see."

Pearl, daughter number four, was a junior in high school. Even though all the sisters were pretty, Pearl was constantly studying various fashion magazines and wearing the latest trends. Pearl had been born with what at that time was called a sleepy eye. One eyelid drooped and she was very self-conscious about it. It was such a sore point to her, she used her makeup and hair-styling talents to cover it up. At times, she turned her head so that eye would be away from whoever she was talking to or when a picture was being taken. Mama Ida chastised her. "Why do you turn away from people when you're talking to them?"

"My eye, Mom."

"No one is looking at your eye. Everyone tells me how pretty you are. That's nothing to be concerned about. Actually, it looks more like you're up to something, which we both know you usually are." Mama Ida responded with a chuckle.

Betty, the youngest, had just started high school. Being the baby of the family, she didn't have many household chores to do because her older sisters took care of them. She spent a lot of her spare time out in the yard with me, so over the years, I got to know her best. Even though all the sisters were athletic, Betty had more time to devote to sports, until she became one of the best female athletes in the city.

Mama Ida always kidded her while she sat on my bench. "One of these days, you're going to have to learn to sew so you can repair your own softball uniform."

"But, Mom, you do it so well. My stitches never hold, you know that."

"They would if you sat down long enough to do it right. You'll have to learn sometime."

"I just don't have time now, Mom. I need to meet Gerrie at the golf course."

"I know, I know." Mama Ida sighed. "Go ahead. I'll try to catch you later."

Betty did eventually learn to sew, but if she ever needed anything complicated, she sought out her mother or sisters for help.

MY FIRST YEAR

CHAPTER FIVE

One day, not too long after I was adopted, Mama Ida sat on her bench, looking through the mail. There was one envelope she stared at the longest before setting it next to her on the bench. Shortly, Gerrie and Betty came around the corner of the house, all dirty from playing softball at the school a couple of blocks away.

"Betty? Why don't you head into the house and clean up. Gerrie? Do you mind coming here for a minute?"

"Anything wrong, Mom?" Gerrie asked.

Mama Ida grabbed the letter to make room for her and pointed at the now empty spot. As Gerrie sat down, Mama Ida spoke. "A letter came today for you in the mail from Congressman Schneider's office."

"Oh?"

"Do you know anything about this?"

"Sort of. May I open it?"

Mama Ida handed her the envelope. Gerrie ripped it open and silently read it, too slowly for Mama Ida, apparently.

"Well?"

Gerrie took a deep breath. "There was an ad in the newspaper to become one of his secretaries. I applied on a whim, thinking there was no way I'd get it, since I'm just out of high school with no practical experience. One of the requirements was for me to come to his office and give them my resume and transcripts, so last week, I stopped in. I gave my information to his head secretary, Miss Philips. She asked me a few questions, had me type several sample pages while timing me, and then gave me a dictation test. I didn't say anything because I only applied to gain some experience with the interview process." Gerrie read further. "Hey. Wait a second. According to this letter, it looks like Mr. Schneider's officially offered me a job." Gerrie excitedly bounced off the bench. "I knew my typing and dictation were good, but not *that* good. Plus I never thought they'd want someone as young as me."

By this time, Papa George wandered out and must have overheard the conversation. He quietly moved behind Mama Ida and put both his hands on her shoulders.

"What, or maybe the actual question is, *where* is this job going to be?" Mama Ida asked in a slightly demanding tone.

"Part of the time in his office in town, and—"

"And?" Papa George interrupted. "Let me guess, Washington, D.C."

"Yes, Washington."

I saw Mama Ida's face start to turn red. "And when were you going to tell us about this?"

"Like I said, I didn't think I had a chance, so I didn't say anything."

I saw Papa George grip Mama Ida's shoulders a bit tighter as he asked, "Gerrie, what are you planning to do about this?"

"I really want this job. It's only offered two years at a time, since that's his office term."

"Where would you stay while you're working in D.C?"

"Miss Phillips said there are chaperoned, women-only apartment buildings and homes we will be assigned to. *Very* chaperoned." Gerrie added quickly.

There was a long, uncomfortable silence that Papa George finally broke. "I'm leaning toward giving you my blessing."

Gerrie jumped up and down. "You mean it? I do have your blessing?"

Papa George nodded. "However," Papa George qualified, "before I give my final okay, I first want to talk this over with your mother better. Then I want to talk to Mr. Schneider. I know being a congressman makes him reputable, but I still want to look him in the eye and check him out for myself."

Gerrie turned and looked at Mama Ida. "Mom?"

Mama Ida continued to stay silent for a bit longer, though the redness in her face finally went away. "I'm still not sure about this, but if your father feels okay about it, and we talk it over a bit more, I will give my blessing, too."

Gerrie gave Mama Ida a big hug. "You'll see. This will be great for me. Imagine me, Geraldine Leinwander, working in Washington, D.C."

Gerrie ran into the house. Papa George sat next to Mama Ida on the bench and put his arm around her. "Are you sure about this, George?" Mama Ida said. "Is it safe for a girl Gerrie's age to run off to a huge city like Washington, D.C.?"

"They're growing up faster than you and I care for, Ida. They have to spread their wings sometime, don't they? You have to admit, of all our daughters, Gerrie, even though she's naïve, is the most practical and doesn't have her head turned too easily."

"You're right about that. I don't think that one will ever slow down enough to even get married."

I'm really going to miss her and all her energy when she leaves. However, I think this is a great opportunity for her to experience life outside of our home.

CHAPTER SIX

Two months later, the air started to cool and the family didn't come outside to play as much as they used to. They still kept me company now and then when they raked the colorful fallen leaves that carpeted the lawn and put them in a huge pile for Papa George to set on fire. Sometimes, they brought out marshmallows, sharpened some sticks, stuck the marshmallows on them, and hovered them over the fire for several minutes. After the marshmallows turned a shade of brown or, in some cases, black, they'd pull them off the stick and stuff them in their mouths.

Usually, Jimmy came down and joined them while they roasted what looked like to me a tasty treat. The first couple of times, they made him stay back away from the fire, but then Gerrie, still home training in Congressman Schneider's Appleton office, found another stick, sharpened it with a knife, and patiently showed him how to make them himself.

"Now, stay back from the fire." she warned. "I got you a long enough stick and the fire's hot enough to roast the marshmallow without you needing to get too close." Jimmy stood back patiently—well, as patiently as a three-year old could, and gradually his marshmallow turned a light brown. Gerrie told him to pull the stick back from the fire and she helped him blow on the marshmallow to cool it. She then gently pulled off the marshmallow, making sure none of the stuffing was left behind, and watched Jimmy shove it in his mouth, with a huge smile on his face.

I wish I could taste the marshmallow. It looks sticky, like my sap.

***

In no time, snow fell, and the girls, along with Jimmy, came out and made snowmen, snow angels, and two large snow forts, which led to several snowball fights. When Pearl and Betty came home from school each afternoon, they sang songs about bells and snowmen, then tried to shove each other jokingly into the snowbanks that surrounded the street by the house. The houses next to mine put up lights around their homes and bushes. Papa George put a wreath on the door next to me and I smelled the sweet scents of chocolate and cinnamon coming from the house. I saw, high above me, lights shining through the windows from the second story until late into the night. I was still much too little to see into the window above me, though, so I had no idea what was going on.

One weekend, Papa George, Gerrie, and Betty left in the car and came back with a spruce tree strapped to the roof. *What's going on here? Am I being replaced? That tree looks bigger than me.* They left the tree on the roof and went into the house.

I looked closer at the tree. True, it was quite a bit bigger than me, but I noticed its roots were missing. Eventually, I smelled the fresh cut wood and sap it was emitting. *What is my family going to do with that tree? Don't they know it won't live with the roots missing?*

Papa George, Gerrie, and Betty returned, unstrapped the tree and began hauling it into the house. *How come you want to bring **that** tree inside but not me?*

"Dad, you don't think this tree is too big to stand upright in the living room, especially with the stand?" Betty asked.

"No, I measured it up to make sure while you were getting the salesman. It should fit just fine, even with the star on top," Papa George replied.

*It gets to wear a star **and** be inside?*

Gerrie added, "I told Mom we were bringing it in and she and Bernie are going to the attic to bring down all the decorations."

It's getting decorated, too? Don't they love me?

They finally got the tree inside and I heard laughter and singing for the next hour.

Probably decorating that tree they love so much.

***

Later that night, Papa George, Mama Ida, Gerrie, Pearl, Betty, and Bernie, who was home from college, piled in one car and Kelly, Lucy, and Jimmy got into theirs. After an hour or so, they came home, along with a few other cars loaded with people who stayed for a couple of hours. They turned on all the house lights, except for the living room. Instead of the normal bright white light that shone through the windows, the lights were soft and colored. I faintly heard more music, talking, and laughter. Once the visitors left, all the lights turned off.

I'm so jealous of that other tree. How come it got to enjoy the party and see what the inside of the house looks like? I thought they loved me, but I'm stuck outside.

It started to snow and I let the heaviness of it sag my branches a bit more than usual.

The next morning, the sun shone bright and the fresh snow sparkled. Papa George came outside early to shovel the walk and the driveway. As he worked his way to the small sidewalk that passed next to me, he stopped, looked me over and said, "Little Ida, you look so sad with all that heavy snow on your branches, and on Christmas Day, too. Here, let me get that off of you."

*Why bother? You seem to love that **other** tree more.*

After Papa George brushed all the snow off of my branches with his hand, he took one more look at me. "Maybe next year, once you're bigger, I can put a string of colored lights on you and show you off to the neighbors."

Well, that made me a bit happier, but I still wondered why they wouldn't bring me in the house. A few days later, I figured it out. The beautiful spruce tree they'd brought inside was now left out on the curb, its brown, dead needles leaving a trail in the snow from the front door to where he lay. *Now I'm glad I didn't go inside. Maybe they **do** love me!*

CHAPTER SEVEN

One Friday in mid-January, there was a huge snowstorm. The next afternoon, Papa George, Kelly, Lucy, Gerrie, Pearl, and Betty came outside to shovel out the sidewalks and the driveway.

About a half hour later, I heard Mama Ida call from the house, "Lucy, Jimmy woke up from his nap and he keeps running around the house, yelling he's going sledding with Aunt Betty today."

Lucy looked over toward Betty. "Did you tell him that?"

"Yeah, he wanted to go yesterday, but I said maybe we could go today," Betty said as she stood up straight from shoveling.

"I think Dad, Kelly, and I can finish up what's left. Why don't you, Gerrie, and Pearl take him over to Riverview Country Club since their hills are only a couple blocks away?" Then she yelled back at Mama Ida, "Mom, do you need any help getting Jimmy into his snowsuit?"

"No, I got it." Then I heard, "Jimmy, you have those boots on the wrong feet and I need to put more socks on them anyway before you go. Here, let me …." Then I heard the door close.

Mama Ida has her hands full with him.

Lucy turned toward her sisters and instructed, "Now, stay on Angel Coffin hill. I don't want you going down Devil's Leap with him." She then asked, "Dad, Kelly, do you have the rest of this? With Jimmy gone this afternoon, I can get some things done around the apartment."

"Go ahead, Lucy. We'll take care of this," Kelly responded. "Are you sure you don't want to join them?"

"I wish, but there's other things I need to do. I'll take him during the week. The snow won't be going anywhere for a long time."

As I watched the girls pull two sleds, with Jimmy sitting on the smaller one, Papa George stopped shoveling, leaned against his shovel and said wistfully. "Wish I was young enough to do that. Oh, well. They'll grow up soon enough. Too soon, if you ask me," he chuckled as he began shoveling again.

I want to go sledding, too, Papa George.

***

They were gone quite a while before I saw them coming down the snow-covered road. As it happened, Papa George was just finishing clearing off the snow from my tiny branches. Jimmy was riding on his little sled with Gerrie pulling him, but Betty was sitting on the larger sled with Pearl pulling it.

Uh-oh. Something must have happened to Betty.

Papa George ran the best he could on the unplowed street toward them.

"Betty, what happened? Here, Pearl, let me grab this from you."

"Thank God, Dad. I don't think I could have pulled her five more steps." Pearl replied in an exacerbated voice.

"Gerrie just gave you my sled to pull a block back," Betty exclaimed as she crossed her arms, initially ignoring her dad's question. "After you both pulled me up to the top, she pulled all the way across the golf course and partway up—"

Papa George had waited long enough. "Betty! What happened?"

As they started toward the house, Betty replied, "We were having a lot of fun with Jimmy. Two of us would stay and help him slide while the other one took a ride on Devil's Leap. We were almost ready to come home when Jimmy begged to take a ride on the big sled. I didn't see the harm in that, so I sat on the sled with my feet on the steering bar. Pearl placed him in front of me and they both pushed us down Angel's Coffin. We were down that hill at least ten times during the afternoon, but didn't go all the way down."

Gerrie said, "There were a lot of people sledding, too, so we were on the edge, next to the No Man's Land area. Betty and Jimmy were going really fast—"

"Weally, weally fast, Gandpa!" added Jimmy.

"Since we hadn't gone down that far, I didn't notice there was drift that created a bump on the hill," Betty said. "I saw it too late and I'm not used to steering with my feet anymore. So we hit it square on and flew."

"Gandpa, I *fwew*," Jimmy said as he flapped his arms like a bird.

"Jimmy, are you hurt?" I saw Papa George stop and look back at him.

"Nah. I fell on my *butt*—I mean my behind, Gandpa. Sowwy, Auntie Pearl. I said butt. I pwomise I will say behind to Mommy. I don't want to get you into twouble."

All of them laughed, including me.

Betty continued, "Fortunately, Jimmy fell in a pile of snow on No Man's Land. No one had slid down that part yet, so it was still really fluffy and soft. But instead of rolling over into the snow myself, I thought I'd be able to safely bring the sled to a stop. Instead, I ended up flipping into the frozen creek and twisted my ankle and skinned my knee. I didn't even feel it at first because I was looking for Jimmy, but I heard him laugh, so I knew he was okay. Then I started laughing, too, until I tried to stand up. By then all of them, plus a few other parents who were there, helped get me up the creek bank and up the hill. So I guess I won't be doing gym for a while."

"Do you think it's broken?" Papa George asked.

"I don't think so. The boots and all the socks I'm wearing helped, but I'm sure Mom will check it out."

I heard a voice from the other side of the house. "George, are they back from sledding yet?"

"Yes, Ida. One injury—"

Another voice joined Mama Ida's. "I told them not to take Jimmy on Devil's Leap. How many Band-aids?"

"None, Lucy. It's Betty. Jimmy's fine, but he might have a bruised," Papa George paused, looked at Jimmy, and then all of them chimed in with "butt"!

CHAPTER EIGHT

Spring brought with it buds beginning to show from the ground and on the trees. I grew a whole new row of shoots with long needles that finally spread out after the bud casings dropped off. I felt so invigorated with the new growth coming from my branches.

But growing and early spring brought with it one of the things I disliked: trimming my branches. It wasn't that it was painful, and I felt great after it was done, but the procedure itself was uncomfortable. Back where I grew up, the farmer'd started trimming us a couple of years before we were sold. He used shears and snipped our branches so we stayed in a conical shape. Every snip felt like a hard pinch, but the initial discomfort went away after a minute or so.

I'd been hoping now that I'd left the farm that my branches were trained enough to keep their shape without the trimming process. No such luck. Papa George and Kelly came out one day with the shears. Even though it still pinched, they took their time snipping and did it gentler than the farmer. I guess I understood that. The farmer had a lot more trees than me to trim in one day and it usually was still very cold out.

***

Gerrie, after seven months training in town, left for Washington, D.C. Two weeks after she left, Papa George was raking the lawn near me on an unusually cold spring morning when suddenly I heard the door slam and Mama Ida, with no coat on, rounded the corner, waving a letter in her hand.

"George, George, we got a letter from Gerrie," she exclaimed.

"Ida, please go back into the house. You're going to catch your death a cold." Papa George scolded.

"I just couldn't wait. Listen to this.

"Dear Family: Washington is such an exciting place. I'm currently rooming with another girl whose name is Bernice. I certainly won't forget that name, haha! I'm learning my new job fast and Mr. Schneider's assistant, who I report to, tells me she's happy with my work and if I keep it up, I might get a raise in a couple months. Once I get more settled and figure out how much money I need to live on, I'll send the rest home to help out the family and maybe put a couple extra coins away for my future."

Mama Ida dropped her arms and looked straight at Papa George. "Bless her heart. Sending us money to help and talking about saving some for her future. She's only nineteen." Mama Ida picked up the letter again. "Okay, where was I?

"Don't worry about anything. Rest assured we are quite well chaperoned, almost too chaperoned for my taste. I should head to bed now. Give my love to the family. Love, Gerrie"

Mama Ida carefully refolded the letter back into the envelope. "I need to make sure everyone gets to read this. I'm so proud of her."

Papa George sighed, then said, "I'm sure the girls will be really excited to read it. Now, Ida, *please* go back inside? You just got over a nasty cold."

I watched Mama Ida turn and walk back into the house. Papa George rested a moment longer against the shovel, then muttered, "I better get this done so I can make sure she gets some hot tea inside her. Actually, that sounds good to me, too."

Sounds like Gerrie's really doing well, but I sure miss her.

From then on, I only heard snippets of what Gerrie told the family because no one wanted to sit out on the bench; it was still too cold outside. After what seemed like forever, we finally got a nice warm day and Mama Ida and Pearl came out and sat by me, Pearl reading a book for school and Mama Ida darning Papa George's socks. Pearl ran into the house to get something and, when she returned, she carried a letter.

"Mom, the postman dropped off a letter from Gerrie. I brought it along in case you want to read it right away."

"Thanks, Pearl. Why don't you open it and read it out loud to me? That way, I can continue to darn your father's socks."

Pearl opened the envelope carefully and began to read.

"Dear Mom and Dad: Guess what I got in the mail today? An invitation to the White House to have tea with Mrs. Roosevelt. Imagine me at the White House! When you write back, would you ask Pearl which of the dresses I brought with me she thinks I should wear? Once I know which dress, I'll see if I can borrow a hat that will match, otherwise I'll have to buy one. I'll also ask around here to see what's appropriate. I think a lot of people get invited to these shindigs, but to be able to see her in person? Wow! Will write about the party in a couple of weeks and hopefully send more pictures of D.C. Love to all and miss you! Gerrie"

"Can you believe that, Little Ida? She's going to meet Mrs. Roosevelt! Pearl, I can't wait to tell the rest of the family."

Pearl said, "She has that nice navy dress with the short sleeves. You remember, Mom. The one with the little white flowers on it and lace on the sleeves?"

"Oh, that sounds perfect. Why don't you write her right away, but before you send it, I'll slip two dollars in so she can buy something she might need," Mama Ida responded as she gathered her darning. They both dashed into the house.

I didn't know who Mrs. Roosevelt was, but she sure sounded important. Since this was the talk of the family over the next couple of weeks, I eventually learned that Mrs. Roosevelt was the wife of the President of the United States.

***

Three weeks later, Mama Ida was outside, enjoying a mild afternoon, when the postman came by. He noticed her sitting there and, instead of leaving the mail where he usually did, walked over and handed a letter to her. "I think this might be from your daughter. It's postmarked from Washington, D.C., and it's too early for tax information. Besides, the envelope is handwritten."

"Thanks, Joe. I've been anxiously waiting for this. A few days ago, she was supposed to have tea with Mrs. Roosevelt."

The postman whistled. "Wow. Mrs. Roosevelt. I sure hope Gerrie still talks to me when she gets back after meeting all those high falutin' people."

Mama Ida laughed. "If there's one person who wouldn't be enamored by all that political power, it's Gerrie."

The postman wandered off to the next house while Mama Ida opened the letter.

Please read it out loud, Mama Ida.

Fortunately for me, she did.

"Dear Everyone: I can't believe I had tea with Mrs. Roosevelt! Well, along with a couple hundred more ladies. It was held in the Rose Garden and while we waited to shake hands with Mrs. Roosevelt, waiters came around and offered hors d'oeuvres. Mrs. Roosevelt has such a firm handshake, but a very warm smile. For once, I couldn't say anything but 'hello'. After we met, we sat at large round tables with white tablecloths and were served tea in very pretty cups with the presidential seal on them. Then we were surprised by President Roosevelt suddenly appearing on the second floor porch and he gave us a wave. I will never forget this day.

"I'll tell you more details when I get home for Easter break. But I can tell you I finally did get that raise I mentioned a while back, an extra five cents an hour. Time for bed! Love, Gerrie"

Sounds like Gerrie had a great time, but the best part of the letter is she's coming home.

CHAPTER NINE

In April, both Bernie and Gerrie were home on their breaks. One day, I heard Bernie whoop and holler from inside the house. Mama Ida was near me, planting her spring flowers, when Bernie came running around the corner. Mama Ida got up from her crouched position and asked, "What's all that hollering you're doing?"

"Mom, I got a letter from DMLC."

"That's nice, dear. What's a DMLC?"

I knew Mama Ida was teasing. That's all Bernie talked about the last time she was home.

I saw Bernie roll her eyes. "Remember? Dr. Martin Lutheran College in New Ulm, Minnesota? The college I need to go to so I can be certified as a Lutheran school teacher. They accepted my transcripts from Oshkosh Teachers College and I'll be going there next year to get certified."

"Oh, that school. How many more years of school will that be?" Mama Ida inquired, more seriously now.

Bernie chuckled. "You were just pulling my leg, weren't you? Just this coming year, since they accepted all my credits. Guess what else?"

"What?"

"Since my grades were so good and they're short of female teachers, they gave me a scholarship. All I have to do is get there."

Mama Ida let out a sigh. "That's fantastic, Bernie. We'll miss you, because that's far away, but I know it's your dream. Wait until your father comes home from work. He'll be so proud of you."

As Bernie rushed into the house to tell her sisters, Mama Ida sighed again and looked down at me. "Well, Little Ida, I guess I need to get used to my girls heading off to live their lives. But," she said as she stood up and put her hands on her hips, "I don't have to like it."

I don't like it, either, Mama Ida.

MY EARLY YEARS

CHAPTER TEN

Over the next couple of years, I continued to grow and my branches filled out. I was taller than the bench now, but still not quite tall enough to see into the windows of the house. I needed a couple more years of growth before I'd be able to peek inside to see what was going on. I was tired of only being able to hear snippets.

During this time, I watched the girls play softball, badminton, croquet, and tag in the yard while Mama Ida and Papa George sat on the bench, relaxing a bit before supper needed to be prepared. Mama Ida always said, "Little Ida, look at my pretty girls. They're getting as beautiful as you are." I straightened up tall every time she was near so she would be proud of me, too.

But I also yearned to be able to play with them, go with them wherever they went, even just into the house. One day, the girls were outside, having a hard time deciding what to play. Gerrie, after almost two years traveling back and forth to Washington, D.C, was back, living at home because Congressman Schneider lost his last election. However, she wasn't unemployed for long. Soon she was working full time in the office at Scolding Locks, the bobby pin factory, in town.

"Want to play tag?" Betty asked.

Even though the girls were older and most of them were out of high school, once they came home after being cooped up all day in a building, they relished being able to throw their high heels into the closet and still play in the backyard. It didn't matter what type of game, even something as simple as tag. They seemed happiest when they were able to run.

"Okay. What should we use as a safe zone?"

Betty looked around.

Pick me, Betty. Pick me.

It was as if Betty heard me. "Why don't we use Little Ida? If you touch her branch, you're safe."

"I don't want you girls damaging her branches." Mama Ida said as she approached her bench, carrying her mending. "I'm not sure she's strong enough yet for your rough housing."

I want to play with them, Mama Ida. I sure hope Betty figures out something.

Betty thought for a minute. She grabbed some mulch from underneath me and outlined a half circle just outside the length of my branches. "Okay, if you step inside the mulch next to Little Ida, this will be the safe zone. Is that okay, Mom?"

"As long as you pick it up after you're done. You know how angry your father will get if he ends up running the push mower over that."

"We will."

After that, the girls let me "play" with them occasionally; touching one of my branches was first base in a softball game, or banging one of their opponent's croquet balls next to or under me so they couldn't take a shot. How I loved it when I contributed to their play, even a little bit. Most of the time, though, I watched and silently cheered them on.

Besides burning off energy running around in the yard, at times they rode their bicycles and I watched them disappear around the corner as they pedaled throughout the neighborhood. The bikes were a variety of colors: red, green, yellow, and blue. All had baskets on the front and a couple had long narrow flat metal racks that friends would sit on and hold onto the pedaler around the waist to get a free ride.

That looks like so much fun. Sometimes I hate being a tree!

***

That summer, Papa George and Mama Ida bought a small cottage on Lake Winneconne, about an hour away from home. I'm not sure why they needed another home, but listening to the family over the next couple months, they had fun riding on a boat, there were bigger fish in the lake than the large river nearby and sometimes it was cooler there than their big house. I didn't blame them. It sounded like fun, but I was jealous that I couldn't tag along. I was lonely when they were gone on weekends. It was too quiet.

Usually, each of the girls had one weekend when they could invite a friend along. One time, Betty brought Mary, who lived a couple houses away, and they must have taken a lot of pictures with Betty's camera. Not long after that weekend, they sat on my bench, going through all the pictures they took. They sure looked like they had fun.

I'm so jealous I could spit sap!

In the fall, Papa George loaded up the car and spent several weekends hunting ducks. Each time he went, he usually brought back a carload.

I guess all those duck decoys he spent time carving and painting were worthwhile.

***

Once in a while on Friday evenings during the summer when they didn't go to the cottage, the family got in the car and drove away. I soon learned that it was custom to go downtown on that day to see new window displays, see a movie, or just meet up with some friends.

Wow, downtown must be busy. I doubt I'll get tall enough to see what it looks like.

If they saw a movie, each of the women would come back with a piece of china that the movie theaters gave away. I overheard them say that each woman who bought a ticket got one piece of china.

That works out well for my family. All but Papa George and Kelly are women.

It did take a while, because each week was a different piece. If they were giving away plates or cups, the whole family saw a movie, and sometimes the girls would go twice during the week. If it was a single piece, like a gravy boat or a cream pitcher, at least one of the girls would go that week. From what I heard, they managed to collect enough place settings for the entire family, plus a couple left over for guests. One time, during a birthday celebration, Bernie came out with a piece of cake on one of the dishes. It had a floral pattern of pink roses with gold leaf trim.

That sure looks fancy for something you get free for going to a movie.

Also, the girls brought out magazines that contained stories about their favorite movie stars that they'd just seen at the movies when they didn't feel like playing a game. A couple of them sat on the bench, while the rest lay on the ground surrounding it. One time, a discussion started on who the best actors and best actresses were was held. I remember one conversation well.

"I love Clark Gable," Pearl said.

Betty chimed in, "I think Errol Flynn is dreamy."

"Don't you just love Jimmy Stewart? He's such a wonderful actor," Bernie added.

"I just saw my favorite actress, Carole Lombard, in *Fools For Scandal*. She is so funny. And you saw Bette Davis in *Jezebel*? How can you think those other guys are better than them?" Gerrie asked as she pulled up and flipped the magazine she was reading on the ground toward her other sisters. "They're both fantastic and I can't wait to see Bette Davis in her next movie, *Dark Victory*."

"I heard on the radio that Clark Gable got the role of Rhett Butler in *Gone with the Wind*. I loved that book. I wonder who's going to play Scarlett O'Hara?" Bernie said.

I remember Bernie reading that thick book, curled up on my bench. She spent weeks reading it because it had so many pages. Wonder how they're going to shorten it into a movie?

"Has to be Bette Davis," Gerrie exclaimed.

"Doubt it. The studio would have to lend her to that studio and *Jezebel* was too similar," Pearl said. "Maybe Katharine Hepburn?"

"Naw, she's too Boston-sounding and skinny. I doubt if anyone would believe her in the role," Betty said. "Besides, I just can't imagine Clark Gable and her romantically together. Yuck."

"Listen to this," Bernie interjected. "MGM is making a technicolor movie musical about the *Wizard of Oz.* I loved reading the *Oz* series of books growing up."

"Do they say who's playing the lead?" Pearl asked.

"Hang on … it says Judy Garland."

"Judy Garland? Why not Shirley Temple?" Gerrie asked.

Pearl laughed. "For a minute, Gerrie, I thought you were going to say Bette Davis. Even *she* can't carry the part of a little girl, no matter how great an actress you think she is."

I really enjoyed whenever the girls came and sat by me. It always made me feel part of the family, even if I didn't understand what they were talking about most of the time.

CHAPTER ELEVEN

Once Lucy and Kelly's second son, David, was born, they needed to move out of the apartment upstairs and into their own home. They bought one about a half mile away. At the time, I thought I'd hardly see them, but the boys and Lucy came by a few times a week to visit and play in the yard.

I'm glad for Mama Ida they're around so much still.

But around the time Lucy and Kelly moved, Papa George sat on the bench next to Mama Ida, a frown darkening his face.

"What's wrong, honey?" Mama Ida asked as she put her crocheting on her lap. "Looks like something's troubling you."

"Today I got offered a better paying job at the factory. A promotion to senior supervisor."

"That's fantastic. Why are you so glum?"

"Well, for the first couple of years, I have to work third shift ... overnights."

"Oh. I guess that does interfere with dinners and evening activities. But we'll manage. It's only for a couple years."

"That's not what concerns me."

"Well, out with it. What are you worried about?"

"I'm concerned about you girls being here all by yourself. With Lucy and Kelly having moved out, there's no men in the house to protect you."

"You're not here during the day and we do just fine."

"That's daytime. I've heard there's been some break-ins lately and not too far from here. And they all happened at night."

"George, we *will* be fine. If it makes you feel more comfortable, I'll tell the girls before they go to bed they need to make sure all the windows on the first floor are shut and locked, even though it's hotter than blazes right now. They can still leave their windows open on the second floor. That should be safe."

"Well, I guess that *would* make me feel better. Just promise me you'll double-check both the windows and doors every night."

"I promise," Mama Ida said as she crossed her heart with her hand.

***

About a month later, it was almost dawn when something woke me up. I looked around and saw someone in dark clothing coming out of the shed.

Who is that? It's not Papa George's time to come home. Wait, I don't remember Papa George saying anything about locking the shed to Mama Ida.

The mysterious man walked over next to me and put the ladder against the house so it reached one of the girls' bedrooms.

What are you doing? Stop it! Don't hurt my family. Geez, I wish I could do something. I'm not even big enough to drop a pine cone on him. I'm so useless!

He'd just stepped on the fourth rung of the ladder, when I heard a familiar voice.

"What the hell are you doing? Get down from there!"

The startled man jumped to the ground without touching any rungs on the way down. He was able to collect himself quickly and took off down the street. Papa George gave chase to the end of the yard, but let him go. I saw lights come on, and soon Mama Ida opened the window.

"George, what's all the commotion? Why are you home so early?" Then she looked around. "What's that ladder doing on the side of the house?"

"Ida, let me catch my breath. I'm not as young as I used to be. Whew, okay. There was a man trying to climb into Betty and Gerrie's bedroom window. He ran off once I confronted him."

"Who was it?"

Papa George laughed. "We weren't properly introduced and I couldn't catch him." He looked toward the shed. "I see the shed door open. That's where he got the ladder. Guess we better make sure that's locked up, too, at least for the time being. I'll call the police tomorrow. Or I guess I mean later this morning when I get up."

"Dad, are you okay?" Betty asked, as I saw her head, followed by Gerrie's, poke out of the above window.

"I'm fine. You both go back to bed now. We'll explain later."

"George, why are you home so early, anyway?"

"Lucky for us, one of the machines broke down and nothing can be done about it until eight in the morning, when the head maintenance man comes in. So the plant manager gave us permission to leave early."

"Well, come in and I'll make us a pot of coffee. I wouldn't be able to go back to sleep now if I tried."

"Sounds great, Ida. First let me put the ladder back in the shed."

I wish I could have done something. I feel so useless, being such a little tree.

***

A few days later, the windows were open and I overheard Papa George and Mama Ida discussing the almost break-in.

"I have something for you," Papa George said.

"It sure doesn't smell like flowers or candy. What do you have in that box?"

"It's something to keep you and the girls protected."

There was a pause in the conversation.

*What's he giving her? I wish I could see inside. When am I **ever** going to get big enough to see in that window above me?*

I didn't have to wait long to hear an answer.

"George, that's a pistol! What am I going to do with that?"

"If there's an intruder in the house, I want you to point the gun at him. Move this latch and it will be off safety. I have one bullet loaded, but only take it off the safety and fire it if it's absolutely necessary. Just having the gun pointed at them should scare off any vagrants trying to steal a quick couple of bucks."

"Where can I keep it? I'm not worried about the girls, but Jimmy and Davey are pretty curious."

"Good point. I need it handy for you, but out of their prying eyes. Say, what about in the back of your top dresser drawer? I highly, highly doubt, once they open that drawer, they'll be digging in there."

"My *underwear* drawer? George Leinwander, what a suggestion."

"I know if I was their age, there's no way I'd dig in *that* drawer."

"Fine. I'll put it in there. But I'll wrap it up in one of my old girdles, just in case."

CHAPTER TWELVE

June 26, 1939. I remember it vividly. It was the first day I finally was able to reach past the windowsill and peek into life inside the house. I was beginning to get sick of always hoping to hear something. It was also the day I saw Pearl get into trouble.

The window I was able to look into belonged to the living room. There was a large, burgundy mohair couch against one wall, a low table in front of that, and a couple of upholstered chairs with footstools in front of them. The backs of both the couch and the chairs were topped with dainty white lace doilies that I'd witnessed Mama Ida diligently make while sitting on our bench. There were lamps next to the couch and in between the chairs. There were a couple scenic pictures on two of the walls, and there were what looked like framed family photographs. To my right, there was a doorway that led to a different part of the house that I couldn't see.

I am sooo excited I can see my family inside the house now. I can't wait until I get tall enough to reach the second floor.

Pearl had a different sense of humor, but, from what I overheard of the other sisters talking, it wasn't especially appreciated. They complained about her short-sheeting their beds, putting ice cubes down their backs, spraying water on them with the garden hose when they walked around the corner of the house, and other things. She steered clear of Papa George and Mama Ida with this humor of hers. At least she had so far.

On that particular day, however, Pearl chose to use her humor on Mama Ida.

"Pearl? You need to do the ironing before you go downtown to Woolworth's."

"But, Mom, I told my friend Hazel I'd be there in half an hour." Pearl glanced at a basket filled with clothes and pointed at it. "This is going to take me all day."

"It will not, if you stop complaining and start ironing. I'm sure you can be out of here by two o'clock."

"But, Mommmmm."

"No *buts*, young lady. You should have checked with me first before making plans."

Mama Ida left the room. Pearl looked at the basket, sighed, and stomped toward a small door I hadn't notice before, opened it and pulled out a narrow board. Pearl grabbed something at the bottom of the board, yanked, and out popped a couple of legs that let the board stand on its own. She went back, reached into the space the door had previously protected, and pulled out a metal object with a cord dangling from it. She plugged the cord into a spot on the wall, set the metal object upright on the board, sat in one of the chairs, and was momentarily lost in thought. A smile suddenly came across her face. She stood and quickly touched her finger on the flat part of the metal object.

"Ouch! Guess it's hot enough now to do the ironing." She grabbed a shirt out of the basket, placed it on the board and started running the flat part of what must be the iron on the shirt. I saw a twinkle in her eye, just like her mother's. Then she started to sing. "The old grey mare, she ain't what she used to be, ain't what she used to be, ain't what she used to be. The old grey mare, she ain't what she used to be, many long years ago."

It didn't take too long for Mama Ida to come back into the room, along with Betty and Gerrie. The two sisters started to laugh hysterically. Mama Ida didn't look amused.

"Pearl, did you sing something?"

"I'm not sure I know what you're talking about. Yes, I was singing a song I love while I iron. What's wrong with that?"

"You love *The Old Gray Mare*?" Mama Ida asked with one eyebrow raised. "Why?"

"You really want to know why?"

"Yes, Pearl. Yes, I really do."

"'Cause it reminds me of you."

"Uh-oh," both sisters in unison.

By this time, I'd learned that Mama Ida was a little sensitive about her age.

This is not going to turn out well for Pearl, I'm afraid.

Mama Ida's mouth popped wide open, but at first she didn't say anything. Then her face turned beet red. "Young lady. You will march yourself right upstairs to your room and wait until your father comes home. You might as well tell your friend Hazel you will not be meeting her at Woolworth's for at least two weeks."

As Pearl slowly made her way out of the room, she turned toward her sisters, smiled, and said, "Well, at least I got out of ironing."

Oh, Pearl, what would the family do without you?

CHAPTER THIRTEEN

One day, when Jimmy and David were over playing in the yard, they found a baby squirrel and brought it to Betty, who was sitting on the bench next to me, taking a small break from playing with her nephews.

"Aunt Betty, we found this baby squirrel by the garage. What should we do?" Jimmy said.

"Let me see him," Betty said. She was eating some peanuts and put one in the flat of her hand and held it next to the squirrel's mouth. "Let's see if he'll eat it. If he does, I think he'll be able to live on his own."

At first, the squirrel was too frightened to move, but apparently the smell of the peanut by his nose was too tempting. He slowly started stretching out his body bit by bit, inching closer and closer to his goal, his nose wiggling as he sniffed, but it seemed he still wasn't feeling very secure about the predicament he was in. From what I've seen, though, the lure of food almost always overtakes common sense and he finally started nibbling on it.

"Well," Betty told her excited nephews, "he should be able to live on his own. But just in case, I'll throw a few peanuts and seeds under Little Ida so Peanut knows where he can find some food."

"Peanut?" her nephews chimed together.

"Well, what else would we call him?"

Both of the boys readily agreed with her as she gently placed him under my branches. At this point, I'd grown to where my top reached the halfway point of the first floor windows. He scurried up my tree trunk and, even though I was still on the smallish side, I gladly let him find a hiding place. It tickled as his tiny claws gripped my trunk. Soon, he found the perfect niche to use as his home.

Every now and then, when Betty sat on the bench by me, she'd have a handful of peanuts that she placed on her lap. "Chitch, chitch," as she made a sound using her tongue against the roof of her mouth. "Here, Peanut. Come here, Peanut. Treats." Peanut came out from wherever he was and crawled onto her lap as she fed him his favorite treat.

CHAPTER FOURTEEN

During that winter, the girls started going to Pierce Park on the other side of the river because a few people created a curling rink. One day, Mama Ida took care of Jimmy and Davey so Lucy could get some housework done in peace at her home. They were playing outside when Jimmy saw Bernie, Gerrie, and Betty heading to the car with brooms. "Hey," Jimmy yelled. "Are you going to clean someone's house with all those brooms?"

Betty stopped and walked over to her nephews. "We're going curling," she said.

"Curling? You're going somewhere to curl your hair with brooms?" Jimmy asked incredulously.

Betty and the other two girls laughed. "That would be a sight, wouldn't it, Jimmy? Us with our short hair trying to use brooms to curl and brush it. No, curling is a sport that's played on ice."

"I never heard of it. How do you play?"

"Well, it's a little complicated, but the easiest way to explain to you is …," Betty thought for a moment, then continued, "you've been to the bowling alley before, right?"

"Uh-huh," both Jimmy and Davey said.

"Well, the ice we play on is narrow like that, but instead of bowling pins, it has a target painted on the ice, actually on both ends of the ice. You've seen us play horseshoes. It's like that. Just like you try to get a ringer on the post, you're trying to get your stones in the center of the target to get points."

"Stones? So why do you need brooms?" Davey asked.

"Well, instead of horseshoes, one person slides a large stone on the ice. The brooms are used by teammates to help the stone go either faster, slower, or in a different direction so it goes into the center of the target."

"But—" Jimmy started to ask, but was interrupted by Gerrie.

"Betty, come on. We're going to be late and miss our spot. You know the men will use any excuse to jump ahead of us."

"Okay," Betty replied. "Boys, I'll try to explain the rest to you when we get back later. Have fun with your snow fort."

Betty jumped in the car and I watched them drive away. For a while, Jimmy and Davey continued to work on their snow fort, but eventually Jimmy said, "This is boring. I want to try curling."

"How are we going to do that?" Davey asked.

"Well, the sidewalk over by Little Ida is very icy. We can use that."

"What about the other stuff, brooms and stones?"

"We have plenty of stones. Why don't you go over to the driveway and pick up the biggest stones you can find? I know where Grandma keeps her new broom. It's just inside the door, so I can quick grab it. I'll be really quiet, so they won't think we're done playing and want to come in," Jimmy answered with a smile.

Uh-oh. I remember Mama Ida giving the girls strict instructions not to use her new broom for their curling and told them they had to buy their own. Jimmy and Davey are going to be in big trouble if Grandma catches them.

I watched Davey hurry to the driveway and begin to look at stones as Jimmy rounded the corner of the house toward the door. After Davey found what I guess were suitable stones, he came over by me and stood by the sidewalk. Soon, Jimmy came back with Grandma's new broom.

Boy, he was quiet. I never heard the door at all.

"Don't we need a target at least on one end of the ice?" Davey asked.

"Davey, let me look at the stones you picked out," Jimmy said. He picked out one with a sharp edge. "I'll use this one to carve out some circles in the ice."

"You're the smartest person I know, besides Mom and Dad," Davey exclaimed.

I watched as Jimmy got on his knees on one end of the icy sidewalk and drew several circles. "I don't know how many circles are on their target, but I think five will do it."

Then Davey handed the six large stones he'd found on the driveway to Jimmy for his approval. "Do you think these will work?" Davey asked.

"I don't see why not. Here, since the broom is really too tall for you to use, I'll do the 'brooming.' You slide the stone on the ice."

Davey and Jimmy stood on the opposite end of where the target was drawn and Davey underhanded one of the stones so it started sliding toward the target. As the stone hit the various bumps and cracks in the ice, it slowed down. Jimmy then ran down the side of the sidewalk, used the broom to catch the stone with the straws and guided it into the middle of the target.

"Bulls-eye," Jimmy yelled and Davey clapped from the other end.

They did this a few times, then Jimmy said, as he was 'brooming' the stone toward the target, "There must be something more to this. It's too easy. We'll have to ask Aunt Betty to tell us more when she gets home."

No sooner had Jimmy said that when I spotted their car coming around the corner. As they were driving past Jimmy and Davey and saw Jimmy using the broom on the ice, I saw their smiles change into frowns. They immediately parked on the road and all three of them jumped out.

"What are you two doing?" Gerrie asked.

"And what are you doing with Grandma's new broom?" Bernie added.

"What does it look like? We're playing curling." Jimmy said proudly. I saw Davey stand up straighter, too. "Aunt Betty, you're going to have to explain to us this game. It's not hard at all. Watch."

We all watched as Davey and Jimmy raced to the one end, Davey slid another stone on the ice and as soon as it slowed down, Jimmy once again raced after it and used the straws from the broom to grab the stone and guide it to the center.

At first, the girls watched silently, but after Jimmy put the stone in the center with the broom, they started laughing so hard I saw tears coming down their cheeks.

Betty was the first to catch her breath. "Well, you've sort of got it, but there's still a few things you're missing."

Bernie turned to Betty. "Actually, from how you described it to them, it's pretty accurate. Why don't we show them how it's done with our brooms?"

Fortunately, at this point, Gerrie took Mama Ida's broom out of Jimmy's hand and held it with hers. Suddenly, Mama Ida's voice came from the window next to me. "Oh, girls, good, you're home. Will one of you walk the boys back to Lucy's? That way she doesn't have to trudge back over here to get them. What are you doing?"

"Oh, just showing the boys a little bit about curling, weren't we?" Betty answered.

"Yeah, Grandma. It sure looks fun. Right, Davey?" Jimmy said as he poked his elbow into Davey's side.

"Uh, yeah, Grandma. Sure looks like fun."

"Okay, but if you're going to try and play that, use one of your aunts' brooms. Don't use my good broom. Promise?"

"We promise," they both said.

Betty said, "I'll walk these two rascals back home. Gerrie, will you put my broom away?"

"Um, sure. Bernie, why don't you give me your broom, too, and go with Betty? I'll put all of them away together," Gerrie said, and I saw her wink at the boys.

Bernie handed over her broom and, with the three brooms, Gerrie was able to camouflage Mama Ida's broom with them. Then she rounded the corner to the opposite side of the house from where Mama Ida was at the window. I guessed she hoped she could get the broom back before Mama Ida noticed.

Betty grabbed Jimmy's hand and Bernie took Davey's and they

walked off to Lucy's house, chatting all the way.

Curling looks like it's fun. I hope they set something up around here so I can see what they actually do. I'm sure if it's a physical sport, the girls will all be good at it.

54

CHAPTER FIFTEEN

Bernie finished college and got a job in New London, a small town about an hour away. Since it was a bit too far for her to come home often during the school year, she dutifully sent a letter once a week to the family, letting them know how she was doing. When it was nice, Mama Ida sat on the bench next to me and read Bernie's letters out loud. "I know you want to hear what's going on with our Bernice, Little Ida." During the summers when school was out, Bernie always came home. After she helped Mama Ida around the house, she usually grabbed a book and sat on the bench by me or told stories to her nephews. She was the quietest of the sisters, but that didn't mean she wasn't as competitive. Put a ball in her hands and she could be just as determined and loud as they were.

I bet she's a great teacher. She's always so patient with her nephews, even though they'd rather be playing cowboys and Indians instead of sitting still, listening to her read to them. I have to give her credit. She always picks out an adventure story to capture their attention.

***

After Pearl graduated from high school, she got a job at Pettibone's, a fancy department store downtown, in ladies clothing, which was ideal because she was always interested in the latest fashions. She called it a "coveted job" since all her friends were jealous because she got an employee discount anytime she bought anything, including the newest styles. I always knew when it was pay day because she would either be sporting a new hat and dress or wearing the latest shoes. Occasionally, she brought gifts for various members of the family: a new Easter hat for Mama Ida, a tie for Papa George to wear to church, jewelry and scarves for the girls, and an occasional toy for her nephews.

Now that all the girls, except for Betty, were out of high school, sometimes, when the weather was bad, instead of playing games, they turned on the radio or put a record on the record player, cranked it up loud enough even for me to hear outside, and practiced their dancing for when they went to the dance halls and bars. The music of Benny Goodman, Artie Shaw, and Tommy Dorsey wafted through the air. I loved to sway my ranches to the rhythm. My personal favorite was Glenn Miller. His song *In the Mood* made my needles tingle.

Just for a few minutes, I'd like to free my roots from the ground and dance to that.

They waltzed, jitterbugged, and foxtrotted together. Gerrie and Pearl would show Betty the newer dances, so when she went to her high school parties, she was up on the latest moves. Swing, the Lindy Hop, and Latin dances like the Rumba and Samba were some of the dances they tried to perfect. Whenever one of Carmen Miranda's songs came on the radio, they would stop what they were doing and form a conga line. They'd pull Mama Ida out of her chair and form a line behind each other, holding on to the person in front of them by the hips, and kick their legs to the rhythm of the music. They'd snake their way through the different rooms and around the furniture. When the song ended, they'd all laugh, and Mama Ida always acted like she was totally winded from the experience and needed to sit down.

I saw a picture of Carmen Miranda once when the girls were reading their magazines outside. She had a tall hat all made of fruit. That's unbelievable.

***

I heard Gerrie and Pearl planning their dates for Saturday night during the week. Usually, they double-dated. If one of the girls didn't have a date, the gentleman always seemed to have a friend he'd ask along. Most of the time, they left at night, around eight, to go dancing at the Cinderella Ballroom.

I bet the girls have so much fun when they go out.

On Saturday nights, after supper, I usually heard them fight over who would get the bathroom first. Normally, Gerrie beat Pearl to the large bathroom on the first floor. Pearl, not known for her patience, would be pounding on the door within a couple of minutes. Then they'd shout at each other until Mama Ida stepped in and told them neither was going to use the bathroom to get ready if they kept it up. After one was done, she'd run up the stairs and start changing clothes. Occasionally, when the other girl got upstairs, another loud discussion began because both of them wanted to wear the same sweater or necklace. They soon ironed out their differences, I think mostly so Mama Ida wouldn't get mad at them again. Most of the time, however, one girl would offer one of her things because, "this will go so well with the dress you're wearing."

It wouldn't be long after the flurry of them getting ready settled down that I'd hear a car drive up and then some knocking on the door. The girls would hustle down the stairs as fast as their high heels let them and after a few minutes, they all flooded out the door and drove into the night.

A few hours later, when the moon was high overhead, I'd hear the car come back, the girls saying their good nights and thank yous, and entering the house. I always knew it had been an important date night if Betty was waiting up for them. Depending on the weather, I'd hear soft whispered descriptions of the music, dancing, and lights that brought both Betty and I there in our imaginations.

I'm sure Betty can't wait to be old enough to go with them.

CHAPTER SIXTEEN

Betty entered her senior year of high school in the fall of 1940. She grew into a fine-looking young woman, though Mama Ida had her doubts about her turning into a refined lady. Mama Ida was always mending some of Betty's shirts or pants that she'd ripped while playing baseball or tennis or just plain running around the neighborhood. If there was a ball involved, that was really the only thing Betty was interested in. Mama Ida managed to tie her down long enough to learn to cook simple things and thread a needle, but that pretty much was it. "Heaven help the man she ends up marrying," Mama Ida frequently said as she patched yet another hole in her daughter's pants.

During the week, I saw Betty racing up the hill after school and hurrying through chores so she could get at least one game of softball or tennis in before daylight was gone and supper was on the table. After supper, she quickly cleared off the table so she could finish her homework before bedtime. She didn't like school very much, but she was fascinated with numbers. She took all the secretarial courses her high school offered and was one of the top students in her class. Always, though, her first love was sports.

***

One May day, Papa George and Betty walked toward the large shed where the car, which the family always called "the Packard", was kept.

Oh, boy, today must be the day Papa George is going to teach Betty how to drive the Packard.

When I was younger, I'd see him teach both Gerrie and Pearl, but I was too young to understand the importance of it. During these last couple of years, I'd noticed that when families came to visit, the man always drove, and if a lady was visiting Mama Ida, she was dropped off. Even Mama Ida never got into the driver's seat. So I came to the conclusion it was a huge honor that Papa George trusted his daughters enough to teach them how to drive and give them their independence.

"Are you sure you're ready for this, Betty?"

"I have to be. Our softball team has quite a few games on the north side of town and I'll need to pick up Gerrie from work, since it's on the way."

"Bernie knows how to drive. Why can't she take you?"

"You forget, Dad. She's on a different team and they don't play on the same diamond we are. Well, except when we play against each other and I don't want to ride with her then. We're enemies that day."

Papa George shook his head. "Sometimes you girls are too competitive for your own good."

"All's fair in love and softball, Dad."

"Okay, okay. I'll back the car out of the garage first. Backing out of the garage will be your last lesson. I don't want you to be so excited on your first day that you forget to put the car in reverse."

I watched Papa George go into the garage and soon, the big black Packard came slowly into view. Once the car was fully outside, Papa George got out while it was still running, and motioned Betty to replace him at the wheel. He then circled the car and got in the passenger front seat. Through the window, I watched him lean over and point to things in front of Betty, sometimes at eye level and, other times, down toward the floor. Then I saw Betty pull on something in front of her and the Packard started to go backward into the road at a snail's pace.

Once it turned onto the narrow road, the car stopped and then gently began to roll forward, toward the ninety degree turn of the road. And then I couldn't see them anymore.

If I'm remembering correctly, when Mama Ida brought me home, not far past the curve there's a steep hill. I sure hope Betty manages that.

Soon, I saw them coming back up the narrow street with the hill — backwards.

I remember now. Papa George always said if his daughters were going to learn to drive, they would be just as good driving in reverse as they were going forward.

Once the car backed past the driveway, it stopped, then moved forward, turned onto the driveway and then stopped again. Betty got out and Papa George took her place in the car and drove the Packard into the garage. They did this a couple of times over the next week, even once after dark, until I saw Betty backing the car out of the garage.

Papa George said that's the last lesson. She must be doing well.

A week later, I saw Betty get in the car alone, dressed in her uniform and carrying her softball equipment, and drive away.

***

In early June, the family set up the backyard for a huge party. When Betty came outside, she was wearing a fancy dress and high heels. When her best friend from down the road, Mary, arrived, they both put on blue, plain gowns over their beautiful dresses and carefully placed a funny-looking cap that fit snugly on their heads with a flat, square board on top. Dangling from it were a bunch of colored strings tied together. Mama Ida and Mary's mother stood in front of me and took pictures of the two girls standing together. Soon, they left in their cars and were gone for a couple hours.

After the family came home, they hung a banner saying *Congratulations Graduate!* The whole family brought out a ton of food and filled up one of the tables. Gerrie and Bernie set up both the croquet and badminton sets. Papa George sat on the steps for the separate apartment entrance and made ice cream. Lots of people showed up and brought gifts for Betty.

After everyone ate, Mama Ida sat down on my bench and started wiping her eyes with the handkerchief Pearl had given her on Mother's Day. Betty saw her looking sad and knelt beside her on the ground. "Why are you crying, Mom?"

Yes, why, Mama Ida? This is a great party. Betty looks happy and is getting presents.

"Because you're my baby and now you're all grown up. I'm so proud that all five of my girls were able to finish high school. Many families around here can't say that. I'm also really happy you did so well in your secretarial courses in high school that you got a job just down the hill at the power company."

"Well," Betty said with a smile, "that was the only way I could stay at home, sleep until seven thirty in the morning and still make it to work on time."

"Oh, what am I ever going to do with you?" Mama Ida said as reached down and gave her a big hug.

Even though none of the girls are in high school anymore, I'm so happy for Mama Ida that most of them are sticking close to home. I'm happy for me, too.

CHAPTER SEVENTEEN

While working downtown, Pearl met an extremely handsome young man named Len. He was tall, thin, and very dashing. To me, they looked like a perfect match. He started coming regularly to Sunday dinners and was the only man who picked up Pearl to go on dates in a fancy-looking car. They dated about three months before they were engaged.

A little too fast, in my opinion.

I know I wasn't the only one who felt that way. The day after Pearl and Len made the announcement to the family, all the girls, except Pearl, who undoubtedly was off showing her engagement ring to her friends, were outside, pulling rhubarb out of the patch.

"I can't believe they're engaged already. They've only known each other a couple months," Gerrie exclaimed.

Bernie stood up and put her hand on her hips. "Well, I think it's romantic. You know the only way Pearl would ever settle down is to be swept off her feet. Len's so handsome and kind, plus you know how impulsive she is."

Lucy, who'd stopped by to get some rhubarb for her family, chimed in. "Marriage isn't a romantic tryst. It's hard work and takes a lot of compromising and it certainly helps if you know the person. I hope she isn't getting married just because a lot of her friends are."

Betty said, "I think you're wrong about that, Lucy. She *is* impulsive, but when it comes to her life, she doesn't usually do what others are doing. Now that I've met Len, I can't imagine her with anyone else. He seems to have a good head on his shoulders and he has a lot of patience. Maybe she knows he's the one. And why wait if he is? It does sound like they're not going to get married until next fall anyway. That should be long enough in case one of them changes their mind."

I hope you're right, Betty.

***

During the summer and fall of 1941, I saw the girls rush to and from work and then off to their softball games at night. Jimmy especially seemed enamored with Betty. Whenever he was at our house, I heard him begging Aunt Betty to play catch with him. Bernie was home again for the summer and helped Mama Ida around the house while Betty and Gerrie were working, but she also left with them after supper to play softball or golf. Didn't matter what the sport was, once they learned it, they outplayed all the other girls and quite a few of the boys, too. Even if they faced off against each other occasionally, they always made up in time for Sunday family dinners.

Oh, how I loved Sundays. Almost every Sunday, the entire family, whoever was in town, got together on Sundays after church.

First, the family went to their church, St. Paul Lutheran, early in the morning, wearing their best clothing.

That place sounds wonderful. I doubt I'll ever get to see it, though.

Once church was done, they came home and changed into their regular clothes. Then, Mama Ida, along with Bernie, when she was home, Gerrie, and Pearl worked on making a huge dinner. Lucy and Kelly came, with their family in tow, bringing with them another part of the meal. Betty usually set the table and then took off to play with her nephews in the yard. I could smell meat, vegetables, rolls, mashed potatoes, and gravy through the window. After a while, apple pie or rhubarb tart aromas started mingling in with the rest.

If it was a holiday, there seemed to be special activities during the day. At Easter, colored eggs were hidden throughout the house for the older people, and there were baskets for the grandchildren. I could always tell when someone couldn't find their egg. Whoever found the unlucky searcher's egg while hunting for their own would start to sing using la-la, softly at first and either decrease or increase the volume, depending on how close or far away the other person was to their target. By the time the offending person finally found their egg, everyone was la-la-ing so loud, I'm quite sure the neighborhood heard them.

On the Fourth of July, the family brought out food and picnicked in the backyard near me, then either played badminton or croquet instead of staying inside and playing cards. When it was dusk, they all piled into their cars and went to town. Not long after it got dark, I saw bursts of color light up the night sky for a few seconds at a time.

Thanksgiving was almost like a regular Sunday, but even more relatives came over. The smell of turkey, mashed potatoes, and pumpkin pies permeated the air after escaping from open windows from the kitchen. With all the cooking and people, there was enough hot air that the windows usually were open.

Christmas became my favorite holiday. Even though my initial encounter with a Christmas tree had traumatized me a little, once I grew bigger, Papa George always brought out some colored lights to decorate me. Dutifully, each day when it got dark, he came outside and plugged them in. It wasn't much, but I felt a bit warmer, although maybe that was more from the attention than the lights themselves.

Now that I was tall enough to look through the window, I finally saw all the decorations I'd heard the family talk about during my first few years. The living room, which really was the only room I could see, was decorated with candles on a couple of tables. Red and green doilies replaced the usual white ones that hung decoratively over the tops of chairs and couch. Green garland with tiny red bows tied amongst them trimmed the edges of the doorframes. In one corner of the room, where usually one of the chairs was kept, stood the Christmas tree.

That tree, like me, was wrapped with colored bulbs that glowed like precious jewels when the room was darkened. Hanging on most of the limbs were colored shiny balls of various shapes and sizes, which helped the jeweled effect by reflecting the light from the bulbs. Almost every branch was covered in silver tinsel that dangled from the branches like the icicles did from the eaves of the roof. To assist it to stand upright, there was a metal stand that was decorated by a colored piece of cloth. But best of all was the star, placed regally on the very top branch of the tree, pointing up to the ceiling. All of this together, when the tree was the only light in the room, created a magical scene that I never forgot.

Maybe one day, they'll bring the star outside for me to wear.

Christmas Eve, the family gathered after coming home from church and ate a light supper. Then they went to various parts of the house and returned with many wrapped presents that they placed under the tree. Soon after, they went to bed.

Christmas morning, I was always awakened by hearing the girls dash down the steps, hurrying toward the presents underneath the unfortunate tree of the year. Even though they were older, they still enjoyed opening their presents and seeing what everyone else got. The mood around the house was joyous. Even snowstorms didn't bother them. In fact, they seemed to enjoy the snow. They'd build snowmen and fall onto the ground, flail their arms and legs and create snow angels. Usually, there was lots of singing: carols about Santa Claus, being home for the holidays, and the birth of Baby Jesus.

No matter what the Sunday or holiday, once everyone was stuffed from eating and the dishes washed, card games of Sheepshead or Gin Rummy were played or, if it was nice, everyone came outside. The younger ones played games while Mama Ida and Papa George sat on the bench next to me, he with the newspaper and his pipe while she either mended some clothes or worked on a crocheting project. Every once in a while, the girls dragged their parents into a game of croquet. Supper time was usually leftovers from dinner.

I remember one Sunday, though, in the early winter of 1941 ....

THE WAR YEARS

CHAPTER EIGHTEEN

The family came home from church, ate dinner, and start playing cards, all as usual. By this time, I was taller than the top of the first floor windows. The house must have been very warm inside from all the cooking, so the window by me was open a crack. They were listening to music on the radio while they were playing, when suddenly, there was a news bulletin. Something had happened at a place called Pearl Harbor. At first, I thought the radio person was talking about our Pearl, but after listening further, I learned whatever had happened took place somewhere on the island of Hawaii. The family immediately stopped playing cards and huddled closer around the radio. After the announcement was over, they somberly put away the cards and began to discuss where this place was and what it might mean to them. Pearl especially had a worried look on her face and clung to Len like he was leaving her forever.

***

Christmas a couple weeks later wasn't as festive as normal. Sure, I heard Christmas carols and the family hung decorations as usual, but the gaiety I was accustomed to just wasn't there.

I have a strange feeling that our world has changed.

***

That spring, the family had a send-off party for Len because he was going off to The War. He didn't know where he was going, but wherever it was, it didn't sound good. A couple weeks after he left, Pearl and Gerrie were on my bench, writing letters to some of their friends, including Len.

"Gerrie, I've made a decision," Pearl said.

"About what?"

"I decided I'm going to move to Chicago and, hopefully, get a job at a huge department store."

"Why on earth would you do that? Say, was that why you and Len were arguing before he left?"

Pearl shrugged. "While he's gone, I want to move to Chicago. He doesn't want me to."

"Why do you want to move there? You'd be away from us," Gerrie asked with a concerned look on her face.

"I read these magazines all about life and fashion in the big city and I desperately want to experience it. It sounds so exciting and glamorous. Besides, wouldn't you want to come visit me and see the sights?" Pearl responded enthusiastically, her eyes shining.

"Big city life isn't all that it's cracked up to be. It's expensive … *really* expensive to live there. That was my experience in Washington, anyway," Gerrie replied.

"I don't care. I'll work hard. I've studied all the fashion magazines until I'm blue in the face. I just know I'd be good at a huge, fancy department store, like Gimbel's or Macy's. All my rich lady customers tell me I have a knack for being honest with them about what they look good in and what they don't. I just know I'd be a success at it."

Gerrie's voice softened. "It sounds like you've made up your mind. Do you have any kind of a plan? Have you applied anywhere?"

Pearl lowered her head. "No, not yet. I was thinking about writing my old friend, Hazel. She's living my dream down there already. Maybe she could use a roommate."

"Well, if that's what you really want to do, you should go down to Woolworth's on your lunch break and read the want ads in the Chicago Tribune." Then Gerrie reluctantly sighed and added, "If you find a couple jobs you want to apply for, I'll help you put your resume and cover letter together."

Pearl grabbed her hand. "Thanks, Gerrie. I knew I could count on you to help. Just one more favor?"

"What?"

"Don't tell anyone just yet. You're the only person besides Len that I've mentioned this idea to. I want to make sure I have everything pretty set before I say anything to Mom and Dad. I don't want anyone stopping me."

Gerrie leaned in and hugged Pearl. "Nope, I won't tell a soul."

I won't either, Pearl.

***

A secret like that wasn't going to stay secret long and I could tell Mama Ida thought something was up with Pearl. Eventually, Pearl did break the news of her wanting to move to Chicago. Both Papa George and Mama Ida tried talking her out of it, but Pearl was persistent. However, she didn't get a job offer right away.

I personally hope she doesn't move to Chicago. Life around here without Pearl? How dull would that be?

One day, though, toward the end of May 1942, Pearl came out by

Mama Ida, who was weeding the vegetable garden, and sat on the bench. "Mom? I got a letter back from the Human Resources Department at Gimbel's, in Chicago, and they have a job opening. I need to get there next Monday for a job interview. Don't worry, I wrote my friend, Hazel, and she said she needs a roommate to split costs with. So I'll stay with her during the job interview and if I do get the job, I have a place to live."

"You know your father and I are totally against this, and I believe you told me Len said if you moved to Chicago, you might as well give him his ring back," Mama Ida said.

"Mom, I'm desperate to experience a big city, even if it's only for a little while."

Mama Ida looked at her beautiful, ambitious fourth daughter. "I know you are, honey, but are you willing to risk your relationship with Len over this? Maybe once he's back, you can move there?"

"Len wrote me that once he's back, he wants to start a family and just be home. He says he'll have traveled enough and wants a little house and to just stay put in Appleton."

"What does Len say about *this*, exactly?" Mam Ida looked into Pearl's eyes.

"He exactly wrote that if I move to Chicago, we're through. He doesn't want me gallivanting around, going on dates with other men — which I have no plan to do. But who knows how long he'll be gone, Mom? He might never come back. I just have to do this for me. I'm not looking to find anyone else. He doesn't understand my desire to experience this life. I think he's afraid I'll like it too much and want to stay there. He doesn't want to live in a big city. I'm not married to him, and just because he doesn't like something isn't going to prevent me from doing it if that's what I really want," Pearl said in a stubborn voice. Then she slapped a pack of cigarettes in one hand, and pulled out one with the other, which she promptly lit up.

I don't know, Mama Ida. She might be harder to tame than Betty.

Mama Ida sighed. "You're old enough to make your own decisions. I just hope you're not throwing away a wonderful man on a whim. And what did I say about smoking? That's not ladylike."

Pearl glowered at her mother, but took the cigarette out of her mouth, dropped it on the sidewalk, and used the toe of her shoe to rub the flame out. "It's not a whim, Mother. I just have to get out of this town and go somewhere exciting. Also, most of the women I know, except my sisters, smoke. You won't let me smoke in the house, so this is the only place here I can."

Mama Ida at first stared back at her, but then her voice softened. "Do you have enough money for the train and to get settled?"

"Since I'm not getting married anytime soon, I'll use the money I was saving for that. Besides, in a few months, working there at double the wage I get here, I'll be able to replace that money quickly."

Even though the house won't be the same without Pearl, I can just see her in a fashionable dress, complete with high heels and hairdo. All those ladies she'll be helping shop there will be so lucky. Watch out, Chicago, here comes our Pearl.

Pearl got the job and moved to Chicago about a month later. Over the next couple of years, Betty and Gerrie took the train to Chicago a few times to visit her. Bernie, on her minimal teacher's salary, was able to go once. Pearl also wrote Mama Ida at least once a week and sent picture postcards of Chicago. While Mama Ida read them on the bench, I peeked over her shoulder and saw buildings that were taller than any trees I knew of.

Wow, even the buildings I saw from Gerrie's postcards from Washington, D.C., weren't that tall.

CHAPTER NINETEEN

One by one, other male friends and former classmates of the girls also left for the war. During the summer, Betty, Gerrie, and Bernie sat by me and wrote letters to them. They did receive letters back, but some of them had words cut out and looked like lace patterns. I thought it was funny, but they always ran into the house to look at a map they'd set up in the living room to follow news of the war.

I guess the more cut-up the letters come, the more danger their friends are in.

***

Not long after Pearl Harbor, I heard the family talking about needing to ration. First, rubber items, like tires, were rationed. Even when The Packard had a flat tire, Papa George had to scrounge up a patch to fix the hole. No new tires were available. Then it was items made with silk, especially nylons for the girls. Now, I don't actually know why the girls felt these were a necessity, but they spent extra time drawing lines to simulate nylon seams on the back of their legs, using their mascara wands, to give the impression they were wearing nylons. They tried to decide whether the line should be exactly straight, starting with their heels, up past their calves, all the way to their mid-thighs, or be slightly crooked, which might make "wearing" the nylons more realistic.

I'm not sure why they bother. Everyone knows they're fake anyway.

Next came the rationing of some food items. Mama Ida was fit to be tied because sugar was scarce and costly. A neighbor a couple doors down had a pear tree, another had a cherry tree. They helped each other out and traded fruit so each family had a variety. Also, Mama Ida made more applesauce and used that as a substitute for sugar in some of her baking recipes.

It never matters to me what Mama Ida uses, everything smells delicious.

Gasoline was another rationing item that hurt the family. It limited trips to the cottage. Fortunately, neither Papa George nor Betty needed to drive to work, so they were able to save some of the gas ration stamps for Papa George to use for hunting trips to the cottage. Since buying meat was another ration item, the ducks, partridges, fish, and deer he brought back were a blessing.

***

Pearl wasn't the only family member to move to a big city during the war. One day in September 1943, Lucy stopped over with the boys. They played in their sandbox while she and Mama Ida sat on the bench watching them.

"Mom, Kelly and I've made a decision and I know you and Dad aren't going to like it much," Lucy said.

"Oh?"

"With Kelly being disqualified from entering the service because of the effect rheumatic fever had on his heart back before we were married, we made some inquiries and he was able to find a good job at a factory … in Detroit."

"Detroit? As in Michigan?" Mama Ida said. "When? What are you going to do with your house?"

"We already have a buyer for the house. Mom, I'm sorry, but it's good money. Much more than Kelly can make around here. It's at a factory that makes rubber tires for airplanes. We're planning on leaving next month, so we can settle in before the snow starts to fly."

"But you'll miss Thanksgiving and Christmas."

"Mom, we're going to miss a lot of holidays, but we'll write often and call when we can. Once we've been there a while, we might get to take time off to come back for a visit."

Mama Ida sighed. "I know I'm being selfish, but I'm going to miss you all so much. You better take lots of pictures to send us so I can keep track of my boys." She nodded toward the sandbox where they played, oblivious of the conversation.

"Thanks, Mom. I knew you'd understand," Lucy said as she hugged Mama Ida.

Just after Halloween, Lucy's family stopped by for a last minute good-bye, their car loaded with boxes and a trailer attached holding still more. The family hugged and cried. I saw Papa George give Kelly an extra rationing stamp. All too soon, they got back in their car and left.

I am so going to miss them, especially the boys. I hope Mama Ida reads some of their letters by me.

CHAPTER TWENTY

One beautiful spring day in 1943, Betty raced over to Mama Ida, who was sitting by me, with a letter in her hand. *With how excited she is, I thought. Maybe one of those soldier boys she wrote to told her he loved her.* I should have known better.

"Mom, Mom, I got invited!"

"Invited where? To a party? Is one of your friends coming home?"

"No, Mom. Don't you remember me telling you about that man who watched us play softball a couple weeks ago?"

"Vaguely, but you tell me a lot of things about softball I don't really understand."

"Mom. I told you he was a baseball scout. I guess Mr. Wrigley, you know, the guy who makes the gum in Chicago, is putting together a girls' baseball league to fill in for the men's teams while the war is going on. This scout thinks I'm good enough to make one of the teams."

"Of course you are, sweetheart. Where are they going to play around here?" Mama Ida asked, sounding cautious.

"It wouldn't be here, Mom. The tryouts are at Wrigley Field in Chicago. Let's see what the letter says." Betty paused, reading the letter further. "The teams will be located at Racine and Kenosha in Wisconsin; Rockford, Illinois; and South Bend, Indiana."

I saw the color drain from Mama Ida's face. "No, Betty, I don't think you should go," Mama Ida responded quite fast.

"Why couldn't I stay with Pearl?"

"Well, that would be okay during the tryouts, but it doesn't sound like you'd be staying in Chicago. Those first two towns you said are in Wisconsin, but I know they're both over a hundred miles away."

"But … but, Mom. This would be an opportunity to play sports *and* get paid for it. Don't you trust me?"

Mama Ida didn't speak for a few minutes. I could see she was trying to form the right words not to hurt her youngest daughter. "Honey, of course I trust you. I'm just not sure what kind of situation you're going to be getting yourself into down there. You have no idea about the world outside our town. I don't think a young lady of your age should be on your own, not with what's going on in the world, unless you have to be."

"Shirley Hausen got invited to try out, too. We could go together," Betty pleaded. "Plus, you let Gerrie go all the way to Washington and she was even younger than I am now."

"The world was a different place before the war. Also, Gerrie was with a group of secretaries that were chaperoned constantly, and all of them, including the congressman, were from here." She took a deep breath before continuing, "Well, you're almost twenty years old. I can't stop you if you really want to go. But with Pearl in Chicago, Bernice teaching in New London, and Lucy in Detroit, it's just Dad, Gerrie, you, and me at home. You know, your father hasn't been feeling well lately and the doctor asked him to take it a bit easy. You're such a big help to both of us around the house. Plus, I'd miss and worry about you too much." She smiled a sad smile. "Ach, look at the time. Sorry, honey, I need to go start dinner. This whole thing sounds a bit shady to me and I think your father would agree, but we can talk about it with him after dinner."

As Mama Ida walked away, Betty sat on the bench and started crying so hard the sound got Peanut's attention. He raced down my trunk and jumped on her lap, obviously looking for a treat. Betty stared down at him and wiped the tears from her eyes. He gazed up at her and cocked his head. She chuckled, gently stroked the length of his body, then dug into the pocket of her skirt and pulled out a small piece of hard candy. She gave it to Peanut and, after shoving it in his mouth, he scampered back up my trunk.

Betty's eyes followed him as he scurried up to his nest in my branches, then her gaze rested despondently at me. "I know Mom's right. I need to be here for them. But to get paid to play sports? A girl used to only be able to dream of those things before, but now it's a reality." Betty sighed. "Well, Little Ida, I guess you're stuck with me for a while." She slowly got up off the bench, wiped her eyes with hem of her shirt, and, as she walked toward the house, tore up the letter and stuffed the pieces in her pocket.

Oh, Betty, I'm so sorry. I wish I could hold you. I think Mama Ida can't bear for you to leave the nest.

***

The next week, Papa George and Mama Ida began working on the garden to get it ready for planting. After using the hoes to break up the soil, Mama Ida said, "George, let's sit down for a few minutes."

As they sat, Papa George frowned and said, "Betty didn't say much at dinner last night. If fact, ever since the day she received that invitation to play baseball, she's been so ... far away in her thoughts. I'm sorry I told her I was strongly against her going, but she's still so naive to what goes on in the world. I'm glad she's a daughter who still considers our advice wise."

"I know, George. She asks about why we feel differently about her going to this as opposed to Gerrie going all the way to Washington, Bernie teaching, and Pearl going to Chicago," Mama Ida replied. "It's just different. Gerrie's job was with people from around here and she worked in Appleton several months out of the year. Obviously, Bernie's a teacher at one of our Lutheran schools. And Pearl—"

Papa George interrupted, "Pearl has her own mind and she was going to go, no matter what we said."

Mama Ida shook her head and laughed. "She sure is different. Not exactly sure which side of the family she got that instinct from." Then her face turned serious. "But this baseball thing. What's to become of that? They say it will be chaperoned, but I just think it might be another thing to show off young women to soldiers when they're on leave, just like I hear on the radio about teenage girls heading to big cities and becoming taxi dancers getting paid to dance with soldiers."

Papa George said, "Your instinct might not be far off, regarding something for the soldiers on leave to watch. At work, there was a Chicago newspaper on one of the tables in the lunchroom. It was open to an article about the girls' baseball league, including a picture of the uniform. The uniform was like a dress with a short skirt. It did look like there were shorts underneath, but I'm sure when they'd be running or sliding, that skirt would fly up."

"I can't imagine, the way Betty plays, that would be a comfortable outfit. She'll have bruises, scabs, and scratches all over her legs and arms before the first week would be done. And who's going to fix her uniform? Her? Not if she wants it to stay together," Mama Ida said, looking horrified.

"That's not all. In the article, it said part of the rules were they needed to always have their face in full makeup and their hair done, even when they were playing ball. You can't tell me the men setting this league up are taking their sports skills seriously. In a smaller article, there was an interview with one girl and she got invited to try out, but told the reporter her friend, who was a better ballplayer, didn't get invited because 'she wasn't very pretty and the scout said they were looking for attractive girls that could play ball.'"

Mama Ida shook her head, then finally said, "You know, if this baseball league had been going on for a few years, then it might be okay. We'd know more. And they do say there are chaperones and, from what you said from the article, they have very strict rules. But it still sounds so sketchy to me. I do think the men who are setting this league up will be in for a very rude awakening when they find out how serious these girls—I mean ladies—take this game."

Papa George thought for a while, then said, "I guess if Betty brings it up again and really wants to go, we'll make sure she knows all the facts. With the magazines and newspapers she reads, she'll soon find out more anyhow, if she hasn't already. Still, as exciting as this sounded to her initially, if she really wanted to do this, she'd have gone. I think in her heart she feels she's not ready to leave the nest yet."

Mama Ida replied, "No, I don't think that's it. I think she feels responsible and doesn't want to disappoint us by doing something against our wishes."

"I'm sure you're right as always, Ida. Let's finish working in the garden," Papa George said as he stood and helped Mama Ida to her feet.

I'm glad Betty isn't going away, but I hope she gets to be her old self soon. I don't like it when she's sad and there's nothing I can do to cheer her up.

CHAPTER TWENTY-ONE

Betty never mentioned the baseball league again. It helped that her friend ended up not going, either. Betty became involved in helping with Victory gardens and war bond rallies, along with the rest of the family, plus she still played in all her sports leagues.

However, the war became worrisome for the family. Most of the news on the radio wasn't good until June 6, 1944. That morning, Mama Ida, Bernie, and Betty were weeding the vegetable garden when we all heard Papa George yell for them to come inside. "The radio announcers said there's going to be a major war announcement in a few minutes. I think the Allies finally landed in France."

"We'll be right in. Betty, Bernie?" Mama Ida commanded, "Let's quick get the rakes into the garage so we can listen."

I didn't know too much about the war, but one of the things I did know was the United States was part of the Allies, so when they were doing well, the family was happy. I got to hear parts of the broadcast: the Allies landed in a place called Normandy. Sadly, over twenty-five hundred men died that day, but they successfully captured the beach. According to the announcers, the end of the war was in sight.

I so hope all my girls' friends come home soon, safe and sound.

Even though the Allies successfully landed in Europe, the war still dragged on, both in Europe and the Pacific, from what I gathered from conversations and snippets I heard on the radio.

***

One Sunday afternoon the following February, Betty and Gerrie were clearing the sidewalk and steps by me and began to talk about a picture in the newspaper that morning.

"That was some picture, wasn't it, Gerrie?" Betty said as she threw the snow from her shovel on top of the already sizeable snowbank.

"Where was it taken again?" Gerrie asked as now she tossed more snow onto the bank.

"A place called Iwo Jima. A small island in the Pacific. It sounds like it's an important island to the Japanese, because they're fighting tooth and nail to keep it. I think my high school classmate, Jack Bradley, is in the picture. Some of the guys talking at the Cinderella last night said in his last letter to his parents, he told them he was in some sort of picture that was going to get some PR. It's hard to tell from the picture if it's him or not."

"I'm sure we'll find out soon enough," Gerrie said as she cleared the last bit of snow off the steps. "Let's get inside. I'm cold."

I hope I get to see this picture sometime.

***

A couple weeks later, Papa George and Betty were walking from the garage to the house and seemed to be finishing up a conversation that had started in the car.

"I just think that's great he's in the picture. From what the newspapers are saying, it might even become a monument in Washington."

Betty replied, "I'm not sure, Dad. Jack's a private person, a very private and serious person. It sounds like he and the other two survivors are going to be dragged across the country, promoting war bond rallies."

"Even if he does hate it, at least he won't be in any battles for quite a while. By the time this touring commitment is done and then he has the surgeries he still needs on his legs, hopefully the war will be over. I'm positive his parents are overjoyed that he won't be in harm's way any longer," Papa George said.

"I'm sure they are. I did notice one of the largest rallies is going to be in Chicago on May nineteenth. Maybe I'll check with Pearl if I can stay with her. I'm sure, if I can even get close to them, he'd like to see a familiar face," Betty said.

I wish sometimes I could go inside, even if just to hear the end of some of the conversations.

***

A week later, I finally saw the picture. Betty was reading the article again in the living room. The picture showed a small group of soldiers, trying to put a flagpole in the ground with the American flag waving in the wind. Betty drew an arrow pointing to one of the men on the picture. Next to it she wrote: John "Jack" Bradley AHS, Class of 1941.

This must be the picture they've been talking about for the last couple of weeks. Gerrie was right. That is some picture.

***

Lucy, Kelly, and the boys hadn't been able to make it back since they moved away, but there usually was a letter once a week from Lucy that contained some of the boys' drawings, and they always phoned on the major holidays. Kelly was working hard and Lucy was able to work part time in the factory's office.

"George. We got our weekly letter from Lucy," Mama Ida called as she trotted around the house one day in April of 1945.

Papa George was working on digging spots for the tiny tomato plants that were scattered around his feet. "There you are, Ida. I thought you were going to help me with this."

"Sorry. The mailman came and I got caught up reading Lucy's letter. They're having a baby!"

Papa George smiled. "Well, I guess it's time for me to take a little break. Why don't we sit down and you read it to me? I don't want to get it all dirty before the girls get a chance to read it," he said, showing Mama Ida the grimy palms of his hands.

"Dear Mom and Dad. We're all fine here. Jimmy is doing better in school and Kelly just got a raise. I'm better than fine. I'm expecting a baby! Should come late September or early October. I sure hope we have a girl this time. I love the boys, but at times, they are quite the handful. Unfortunately, that changes our plans of us coming home for Christmas—the baby will be too little to travel in the winter, but I'm hoping for Easter.

"Hope everything is well with you all. I included some drawings by Davey for you.

"Love to all. Lucy"

"Well, I'll be jiggered. Another grandchild," Papa George said as he hugged Mama Ida. As she pulled out of the hug, I saw her face was covered with tears. "What's wrong, Ida?"

"Will this child even know who we are? They live so far away. The way things are going for them in Detroit, I don't think they'll ever come back."

Papa George put his arm around her. "Oh, I don't know. Things change. We'll just hope everything goes well and they can visit next Easter." Then he nodded toward the garden. "You know, Ida, those tomato plants aren't going to crawl into their holes by themselves. Why don't you run the letter back into the house and help me finish this up?"

Mama Ida said, "Fine. Give me a minute. I'll bring out some iced tea. You look like you could use something to drink, Grandpa."

"Thanks, Grandma."

I can't wait until next Easter. I miss the activity the boys bring. Plus, I'd like to see Mama Ida's huge smile again. It's been missing somewhat since they left.

CHAPTER TWENTY-TWO

May 8, 1945 was a momentous day. The war in Europe was over. That man, Hitler, who started the war, was dead, and the Allied soldiers were in Berlin. Church bells were ringing, cars and trucks were driving around the neighboring streets, honking their horns, and people were hanging out the windows and waving flags. Betty and Gerrie recognized some of the men driving and hopped in their cars.

Betty yelled to her parents, "It sounds like there's a big gathering downtown. We're heading down there. Don't wait up for us. Happy VE Day!"

"Have fun, you two," Mama Ida called after them, waving.

VE Day?

As the cars sped away in the direction of downtown, Papa George put his arm around Mama Ida's waist and said, "Now that we have victory in Europe, I hope it won't be long until we celebrate VJ Day, victory in Japan."

I get it. VE Day stands for Victory in Europe.

"I pray this whole ordeal will be over soon. With this going on for three and a half years, will anything be normal again?" Mama Ida said, putting her head on his shoulder.

"Maybe not totally, but, hopefully, a lot more peaceful world than it's been the last couple of decades."

They both walked inside and turned on the radio to listen to more reports and celebrations being broadcast from the larger cities.

I am so glad the war is almost over. I hope Papa George is wrong. I miss the old days. Maybe now Pearl and Lucy's family will come home where they belong.

***

Before the war started, one of the activities the girls liked to do was go to Goodland Field on the west side of town to watch the Appleton Papermakers, a semi-pro baseball team, play. According to them, it was a lot cheaper going to these games than to take the train to Chicago to watch the Cubs. But when war broke out, there weren't enough men to continue the league. Now, since Germany'd surrendered, some of the soldiers began to come home and formed a couple local teams just to start practicing for when the leagues started up again. Word got out and, when they weren't busy with their own sports, they went to the baseball field to watch. One afternoon in mid-July, they came home and found Mama Ida and Papa George sitting on my bench, enjoying the sunshine before dinner.

"Hey, Mom and Dad, you'll never guess," Gerrie said as she raced Betty toward them.

"What? And slow down. You are the only two girls, who are women now, who I see run anywhere outside of a softball field. Geez!" Papa George said with exasperation.

"I won," Betty yelled as she touched Mama Ida's knee.

Gerrie, just having been edged out by Betty, put her hands on her hips and exclaimed, "No fair. I hesitated when Dad was talking to us."

"Sorry, Gerrie. Don't be a sore loser," Mama Ida said as she winked at Betty. "Now, what were we supposed to guess?"

Betty replied, still out of breath, "We saw a bunch of activity going on at the Fuhremann's when we went to the ballgame. You know, the canning company across the street from Goodland Field?"

Papa George's eyes suddenly looked interested. "What kind of activity?"

Gerrie said, "There were several men clearing a spot on the property and beginning to put up large tents."

Betty added, "I recognized one of the builders from my high school class and asked him what was going on. You'll never guess."

"Martians are going to work there?" Mama Ida asked in a serious tone, but I saw the twinkle in her eyes, meaning she was joking.

Gerrie laughed. "Mom, you're closer than you think. It's being turned into a German POW camp."

"You're not serious, are you?" Mama Ida asked, the twinkle disappearing.

"Yep," Betty said. "My friend, Larry, told us they're arriving in a couple days to help finish getting the camp set up."

"What on earth are they doing here?" Mama Ida asked.

Papa George jumped into the conversation. "I'm guessing they're going to be working for the canning company, probably going out to help pick vegetables in the fields outside of town. I read something about it in the newspaper that, all over the United States, they're setting up these camps to help with a variety of menial jobs until most of the men are back from the service. That article also said it was cheap labor for the companies. Since they're prisoners, they won't get paid anything. So technically, it *is* a POW camp. Even so, I'm sure it's better than where they were being kept in Europe. I just didn't realize they'd put one here."

"Are we safe, George?"

"I'm sure we are, Ida. They'll have guards, and besides, the war's over for them and their country. I think they'll just do what they can in order to go home eventually."

Mama Ida sighed. "Well, hopefully, all this war craziness will be done soon."

I hope so, too, Mama Ida.

Betty only mentioned it once more, a couple weeks later, after going to a baseball game. She told Papa George and Mama Ida she saw the prisoners coming back from the fields in a bus. The windows were open and they were singing a German tune she didn't recognize. Betty then told her parents the men waved at her and that she waved back.

"I think they just want to go home. Pretty soon all the fields will be picked and they'll be moving on," Papa George said. "I hope it won't be long before they're allowed to go back to Germany."

I hope they make it home. Even though they fought for the enemy, they weren't the ones who started the war and all I wish for them is peace.

***

Even though the war in Europe was over, the Allies' struggles in the Pacific continued throughout the summer. According to the radio reports, the Japanese were ready to fight to their last man because surrender was viewed as such a disgrace that they might as well kill themselves. And it sounded like they were. Reports came that some of the Japanese pilots were flying into the U.S. battleships instead of going back to their own ships. Papa George said they were called *kamikazes*. The reporters predicted the war could go on for another year or two.

Monday, August 6, 1945, when the girls came home from work, Papa George greeted them at the door. "Hurry! The news reports say we dropped some kind of giant bomb on a city in Japan that totally destroyed it."

Fortunately for me, being summer, the windows are wide open.

"You mean an air raid?" Gerrie asked.

"No, one single bomb. They called it an atomic bomb," Papa George told her.

Bernie, who was working at Gerrie's company like usual during the summer, added, "I did read something about this in some of the science magazines I read for school. I don't understand it totally, but it has to do with atoms splitting using some radioactive material."

"But how could it destroy an entire—"Betty started, but was interrupted by Papa George.

"Shh, the three of you. I want to hear the reports."

The news reports didn't add much more, except to say it was dropped on an industrial city called Hiroshima and about three hundred and twenty thousand people lived there. The next day, it was reported that almost a hundred and thirty thousand people lost their lives.

The Japanese have to surrender now, don't they?

But the Japanese didn't surrender right away. Then, on Thursday, August 9, a second atomic bomb dropped on another Japanese city, Nagasaki, which killed over two hundred and twenty-five thousand people. The following Wednesday, Japan surrendered.

All the soldiers will be coming home soon. Happy VJ Day!

The celebrations were a bit more somber this time around. Everyone was happy the war was over, but all the family, and the newspapers they read, could talk about was *the bomb*. They seemed relieved that only we had this bomb, but they were concerned that other countries, especially Russia, might also eventually get it.

Why can't people get along? Don't they realize how lucky they are? They can go and see different things and learn. I feel sorry for them. This time, I'm happy I'm a tree.

POST-WAR

CHAPTER TWENTY-THREE

Soon, all of the girls' friends came home. This included Len. During the war, he'd written to Mama Ida every once in a while to check on how Pearl was doing. After reading one of his letters out loud from her favorite bench, she turned to me and muttered, "Little Ida, what can I write to him about? Pearl tells us that she loves her life in Chicago. When she visits, or when the girls visit her, she's all smiles. I know he wants to hear that she's back home, having found the error of her ways, but that's just not the case. I love Len and I think he has the patience to deal with her, but I have to go with what makes Pearl happy."

Len eventually stopped writing. I thought maybe he died there. His last letter to Mama Ida had been over a year ago. One day, a car that I hadn't seen in a long time parked by the house. A tall, dark-haired man got out.

Len made it through the war. I'm so happy.

He nervously looked around the outside of the house and saw Bernie cutting some rhubarb. He looked at her for a bit and didn't say anything. Soon, she looked up, put her hand just above her eyes to block out the sun, and screamed, "Oh, Len. You're alive. Mom, Dad, everyone? Len's here."

She ran over to him and gave him a big hug. Soon, the rest of the family came out, smiling, and hugged him. After everyone greeted him, he looked around and his smile turned into a frown. "No Pearl?"

"Sorry, Len. She's still in Chicago, and loving it, I hear," Papa George said.

There was an awkward pause, but then Mama Ida sat on her bench and patted the empty space next to her. "Bernie and Betty? Why don't you get that pitcher of lemonade I made this morning and some glasses? We need to hear all about Len's adventures—that is, if he wants to tell us."

Papa George disappeared around the corner and brought back a few chairs that he placed in a circle by the bench. He and Gerrie sat, leaving chairs for Bernie and Betty. Soon, Bernie returned, holding the lemonade pitcher, and Betty carried six glasses.

They really like lemonade. Wonder why they can't pour some on my roots, so I can have a taste.

Bernie started filling up the glasses, handing the first one to Len. He looked at his feet, passing the glass between his hands a few times before he spoke. "I haven't really spoken about the war to many people yet. I saw men getting their arms and legs shot off and the sounds and cries that came from their lips … well, at least those were the ones that survived on the field. I don't know if they did once they were carted away. One man, a couple yards from me, I saw this head —" Len looked up and saw the horrified looks on all their faces. "Um, I don't want to get into details with you ladies present, but, well, he died right there. One battle I was in, it was so cold some of the guys even froze to death in their trenches. We were in that area over a month between December and January. We started by a little town called Saint Vith in Belgium. Once in a while, we were able to take turns and go into town to warm up and have a hot meal. One day, the German panzers—that's their word for tanks—came toward us. We battled them for several days, but, finally, our commanders had us retreat. We then moved toward Bastogne. I was one of the lucky ones in our unit. That was the one good thing about coming from Wisconsin: I was a bit more used to the cold than some of the guys. We had guys from Georgia, Florida, and Texas. Some days didn't get above zero," Len stopped a moment to take a drink.

During the pause, Papa George asked, "Sounds like you were at the Battle of the Bulge?"

Len nodded.

"Well, we're sure glad you're home," Mama Ida exclaimed as she draped her arm around his shoulders and gave him a squeeze. "It's close to dinner time. Would you like to stay? I have extra pot roast."

"Thanks, Mrs. Leinwander. I'd love to. Outside of Pearl, I missed your cooking the most."

"Girls? Come help me get dinner finished and, Betty, set another place at the table. Let the men relax a bit before dinner."

After they went into the house, it was just Papa George and Len left sitting by me. "I can't imagine what you went through," Papa George said as he lit up his pipe.

"No, I don't think you can. I saw one man trying to get to the medic with his guts in his hands. Fortunately, before he got too far, a German sniper shot him in the head. I just can't …."

"No need, Len. We won't ask anymore. I can tell it's just too painful and there are some things that need to be left overseas … if you can. I'm assuming you didn't come here to see us, did you?"

"No. I was hoping Pearl had come home, now that the war is over."

"Afraid not. It sounds like she's planning on staying in Chicago."

"I love her so much. I only heard from her a couple of times after we broke up, but I can't get her out of my mind. I tried dating some women over the last couple of years, but none of them were right. Do you know if she's seeing anyone?"

"I do know she's been dating ...," Papa George hesitated as we both saw Len's chin drop, "but none of them have stuck around. I don't think she's seeing anyone at the moment, though. Ask Betty, she seems to write and visit her the most."

Len's face perked up at that news. "Well, if Pearl will have me, I'll move to Chicago, if that makes her happy. I still think she'll get tired of that big city life and want to come home." Len looked hopeful.

"Maybe she will. One never knows about her," Papa George said.

"Don't I know it."

***

The windows were wide open one unseasonably warm day in September, so I could see Mama Ida performing her weekly dusting of the tables and furniture in the living room. I heard the phone's rude ringing. She gave it a disgusted look as she hurried over to answer it.

"Leinwander residence ... yes, this is Ida Leinwander. A collect call? Who, Pearl Leinwander? You bet I will. Hi, Pearl. Anything wrong? What? You got *married*? ... Just an hour ago? ... Len? He came down there? Well, I'll be. You're coming home when? In two weeks? Of course, I'll let the family ... you want to surprise them about being married? Okay, I'll just let them know you're coming for a visit. Yes, dear. I know this is costing us. I love you, too, and we'll see you in a couple weeks."

Len must have decided to go to Chicago and convince Pearl to marry him! I can't wait for the rest of the family to find out.

***

A couple weeks later, the whole family was outside when Len's car pulled up. He jumped out and quickly ran to the other side and opened the passenger side door. He reached in and gently helped Pearl to her feet.

As the went toward the car to greet them, Len put his hand up and they stopped in their tracks. "Let me introduce you to Mrs. Leonard Gerrits."

The family raced over to both of them with hugs and handshakes all around. Pearl was dressed to the nines. She wore a beautiful navy dress suit with little pink and white flowers on it. The jacket was longish, but cut so that it fitted her waist and created a peplum at the bottom. She also wore a small hat that was decorated with the same color flowers on her dress, plus a small veil that barely covered her forehead. She'd brought presents for her sisters and Mama Ida from Gimbel's, where she worked.

As they were beginning to go into the house, Betty hooked her arm with Pearl's and asked, "How did this happen? I was expecting to be a fashionable bridesmaid, wearing a dress all the way from Chicago."

"Well," Pearl replied, smiling, "he knocked on my door three weeks ago and just swept me off my feet. He said he didn't care if we lived in Chicago or Appleton, he just wanted to be with me. I knew Mom and Dad wouldn't have been happy if we lived together while waiting to get married, so we just did it."

"Impulsive as ever," Mama Ida interjected as she caught up with them. "Len's a good man, and loves you to pieces."

Pearl's face turned serious. "Yes, he is, Mom. Back when he left, I loved him so much, I was too afraid he wouldn't come back. I don't think my heart could have taken that. So it was easier to just break it off. I was prepared never to see him again, whether he survived the war or not. I'm just so happy he still loves me enough to find me. I'm never going to let him go again."

Pearl and Len stayed a couple days at the house, then went back to Chicago. They'd decided to continue to live there, at least for the time being.

I hope they move back soon. Home is just a bit dull without Pearl around.

CHAPTER TWENTY-FOUR

I heard the phone ring faintly through a crack in the window on October 1.

"Leinwander residence ... Kelly?" Mama Ida paused. "That's wonderful! How's Lucy?" Another pause. "That's great. I know this is costing you, so have Lucy write and send pictures when you can. Love you both." I heard Mama Ida hang up the phone and then shout, "George, Betty, Gerrie ... it's a girl!"

Mama Ida and Papa George finally got their granddaughter. Now I really can't wait for Easter.

***

It seemed like forever before Easter Sunday in 1946 came. It didn't help that it wasn't until April 21. But, just like Lucy promised in her letter, I saw their car park in the driveway the Wednesday before Easter. The boys hardly made it out of the car before I saw Mama Ida race across the lawn towards them.

I've never seen Mama Ida move so fast in my life.

She knelt down and the two boys ran into her arms. I saw both Kelly and Lucy pause to watch the reunion. Then Lucy reached into the front seat and brought out a large bundle of blankets and walked toward Mama Ida. From the opposite side of the lawn, I saw Papa George finally catch up with his wife.

"Mom and Dad? Here's your granddaughter, Sharon." Lucy handed the bundle of blankets, which started to squirm, to Mama Ida. She peeled back one end of the blankets and I heard a soft squeal as a little face appeared.

"Hi, little Sharon. I'm your grandma."

Papa George peeked over Mama Ida's shoulder. "She's beautiful. You know, even though it's warm for here right now, it's still a bit chilly for the baby. Let's get inside." Then his attention turned toward the slam of the house door. "Betty, Gerrie, before you start cooing over the baby, help Kelly and Lucy bring in their bags. I don't think your mom is going to let go of the baby much." He laughed as he grabbed a hand of each of his grandsons.

I sure hope they come back outside soon. I want to have a good look at baby Sharon, too.

They were home for a week. Fortunately, the weather, although cool, was warm enough for the boys to chase around outside with their aunts keeping an eye on them. Mama Ida and Lucy did come and sit on the bench a couple of times with Sharon, or Shari, as they nicknamed her. She was bubbly and laughed quite a bit, although at night I did hear some crying. The Saturday before Easter, Pearl and Len drove up from Chicago and Bernie came home from New London.

Mama Ida is so happy and so am I. The entire family is home.

Since the weather was so nice on Easter Sunday, Papa George hid the boys' baskets outside. He walked over by me with one of them. "I think I'll hide Davey's basket back here behind you, Little Ida. I really want to make this a special Easter for them. I'm not sure how many chances we'll have time to spend with the kids when they're young since they live far away." Papa George wedged himself behind me and the side of the house. "It's a good thing this basket has a lot of brown in it. I'll use some of the dead leaves and needles to help hide it a bit more." He came back out and stretched his back, "Wow, Little Ida. I'm not as agile as I used to be." Then he looked me up and down. "With all the excitement of Lucy coming home and getting the house ready, I forgot to trim you. I still have time. I'll take care of you next weekend after they've gone."

Yuck! Trimming. Thought I'd gotten out of it this year.

***

Not long after Lucy and Kelly returned to Detroit, the phone rang. Papa George answered it. "Hello, Leinwander residence ... Lucy? Something wrong? ... oh ... he's in the hospital?"

I saw Mama Ida enter the living room, wiping her hands on the apron she always wore around the house. "George, is it Lucy?" Papa George held his hand up to her and continued listening on the phone. That didn't seem to stop Mama Ida. "Is it one of the boys?"

I saw Papa George lose his patience and cover the phone, "Ida, please. I'm trying to get the information." Mama Ida's face looked pleadingly at him while she nervously twisted her apron with her hands. Papa George must have noticed. His shoulders relaxed a bit and the receiver went back to his ear as he answered Mama Ida. "Kelly's in the hospital. Now just wait ... Lucy? Sorry about that. Your mother's here, wondering what's going on ... okay, give us a quick call tomorrow to let us know how he's doing. Love you and tell Kelly we'll be praying for him. Bye."

No sooner had he hung up when Mama Ida bombarded him with questions, "What's wrong with Kelly? Accident at work?"

"No. Sounds like the rheumatic fever hit him again. He's really struggling and Lucy says it's day to day."

"What did the doctors say?"

"Again, Ida. Day to day. But—and Lucy didn't say this out loud; I could tell by the sound of her voice—the doctors must not be holding out a lot of hope. I heard the fear in her voice."

"Does she need me to take the train there and help?"

"No, she said Kelly's mom and aunt are already on their way. She called them yesterday ... and before you ask, their neighbor is taking care of the children until they get there. I know you want to be out there to help, but if this is as bad as it sounds, Kelly's mother needs to be there."

"What are they doing for him?"

"Lucy said they have a new medicine called penicillin they're giving him. It's something they're hoping will get rid of the fever. She said all they can really do is wait and see if it works. And that's all we can do, too. Wait and pray."

This sounds really bad. I'll wait and pray, too.

***

After a week of waiting by the phone, everyone's prayers were answered. The new medicine worked and Kelly gradually began to get better. But from what I overheard from the family, he wasn't recovering as fast as the doctors thought he should. To support the family, Lucy went to work full time and Kelly's mother stayed to take care of him and the kids.

Thanksgiving brought more news from Lucy. The window by me was open, I'm guessing because the house was hot from all the cooking. *Oh, I do love those smells.* The rest of the family, including Pearl and Len visiting from Chicago, had just gathered around the table, when the phone rang. Mama Ida, still bringing steaming hot food to the table, was closest to it so she answered. "Happy Thanksgiving. Leinwander residence ... hi, Lucy, how are things going?" There was a long pause, then, "Are the doctors sure that's best?" Another pause. I could see the rest of the family intently listening to the conversation. "How soon ... after the first of the year ... are you going to need any help ... no? Well, I know this is costing you ... give my love to the rest of the family and I'll let everyone know what's going on. Write a letter soon with more details. Love you. Bye."

"Well, Ida?" Papa George queried, "what's going on with them?"

"The doctors feel Kelly needs to be in a place with drier air for a while. He's not recovering as fast as they'd like and they've had success with patients who moved to a more arid climate ... in Arizona. So, after the first of the year, they're packing everything up, selling the house, buying a trailer, and moving to Arizona."

"All the way across the country? Is Lucy going to have to do all the driving? I know Kelly's mother doesn't drive."

"Well, she mentioned that Kelly's brother, Marvin, is quitting his job here and taking the time to help get them and their belongings there. She said not all the details were worked out yet, but that's the plan. Oh, it's starting to feel a bit chilly in here. I'll shut the window before we start eating."

Darn it. I wanted to hear more about what's going on. I don't really know where Arizona is, but it sounds further away than Detroit.

***

Papa George came out a week later to put out all the outside Christmas decorations. He saved putting the Christmas lights around me for last. This year, it was going to be easier for him because whatever little snow we had was melted.

As he was untangling the light string, and saying words I don't want to repeat, Mama Ida came out, moved the bench slightly and sat.

"Ida, what are you doing out here?"

"Well, since it was a warm day for December, I thought I'd get out of the house a bit and see if you needed any help. By the words I'm hearing out of your mouth, you just might." Mama Ida laughed.

"I just don't understand it. Every year, I'm so careful, wrapping these lights up so they won't get tangled. And every year, I waste an hour untangling them when I'm going to put them up," Papa George snarled back.

Mama Ida continued to smile. "Well, I believe it's one of God's tricks to make you slow down."

"I think it's one of his tricks to get my blood boiling. Since you're here anyway, hold this end while I get this part unknotted," Papa George said.

Soon, with Mama Ida's help, the lights were untangled and Papa George started wrapping them around me. The last couple of years, he hadn't started at the top, and this year, with no snow to give him a little extra boost, he only was able to cover the bottom five branches. I guess I thought no snow would be easier for him, but now he couldn't reach as high.

"I guess this might be the last year we're able to put the lights on her," Papa George commented as he located the plug.

No! I like the lights. I feel part of the family celebrating when I have them on.

"Well, George, maybe you'll have to ask the girls to help you. You can use the ladder then."

"But, Ida—"

Mama Ida interrupted, saying, "I like Little Ida all decorated. I bet if she could talk, she'd tell you she likes it, too."

Papa George walked over to the outlet near me and plugged in the lights. They all gleamed softly, giving my branches a glow of rainbow colors. "Well, at least all the lights are working. I'll start putting the boxes away."

Mama Ida asked, "Do you need any help?" I saw Papa George shake his head. "Then I think I'll sit out here a bit. I'll get warmed enough soon making dinner."

After Papa George took the boxes into the garage, Mama Ida pulled out a letter from her coat pocket and silently read it. I saw her eyes tear up and she said, "Little Ida, I just got a more detailed letter from Lucy. I know they have to move for Kelly's health, but why does it have to be so far away? What if they stay there forever?" I'd never seen Mama Ida cry before and there was no one around to comfort her right now.

Sometimes I feel so helpless. There's not even a wind to help me try and brush a limb on her back.

After a minute, she stopped crying. "Well, I got that out of my system. I thought this new letter was going to tell me they'd changed their minds and were going to come home. With Christmas coming up, it's hard to find any alone time so I could finally get the tears out. I'll keep praying that they'll be able to come back soon, with a healthy Kelly. And I'll make sure the girls talk to George about finishing the lights on you. It's getting cold and I'm sure George is wondering what happened to me. I better get inside."

Mama Ida didn't want anyone around to see her that sad? Humans are sure funny sometimes. Little did she know that I was with her the whole time, listening.

CHAPTER TWENTY-FIVE

One winter day in early 1947, a red truck that had a sign that said *Appleton Flooring* pulled up to the curb. A short, dark-haired man jumped out and bounded toward the door.

Who is that? Is the family putting in new flooring?

Someone let him inside the house and I prayed they'd go into the living room where I could see him better.

They did … my lucky day.

He entered the room with Gerrie and Mama Ida. Since it was winter, the windows were closed so I could only watch.

Darn this cold weather.

He sat on the couch next to Gerrie and Mama Ida sat in her favorite rocking chair. The man leaned in close, seemingly paying a lot of attention to Mama Ida. Soon, Papa George joined them, but remained standing, leaning against the door frame. The younger man stood, walked over to Papa George and extended his hand. Papa George shook it and motioned for him to sit.

They talked for a few minutes more. Then Gerrie and the man left the room, Gerrie in front of him and the man with his hand in the middle of her back. Soon they came outside, and, as they drove away in his truck, I saw Betty with them.

Who is this guy and why is he paying so much attention to Gerrie? Where is he taking her and Betty? I guess it's okay because he met Papa George and Mama Ida—but I didn't meet him.

I saw the truck numerous times during the winter and, for the first few times, I saw Betty tag along. However, after a while, it was just Gerrie and this man who went out a couple nights a week.

It took until spring before I finally got the full story. His name was Dick LaBore. Through bits and pieces of conversation over the next couple months, I found out he was from Minnesota and had worked a flooring job in this area for a couple months before the war. After the war, he wanted to buy his own flooring business and found one for sale in Appleton. Because he'd loved the area so much when he was here, he bought it. He didn't know anyone, but he was very friendly, loved to bowl, golf, hunt, and fish. He seemed to fit right in with this family, since it sounded like he'd met Gerrie bowling. After a few months, he seemed to be invited to every Sunday dinner. He was short; Gerrie was about half an inch taller than he, but he had an infectious laugh and his eyes twinkled like Papa George's.

During that spring and summer, whenever they were outside, Dick seemed to always be around. Papa George liked him. Sometimes they went fishing together. Mama Ida, however, seemed to love Dick. Whenever they were together, he always made her laugh and complimented her cooking. To me, it looked like they had a special bond.

I remember one summer day. Gerrie and Dick mentioned to Mama Ida they were going on a picnic at Lake Winneconne. Later, I heard Mama Ida's voice come from the kitchen. "Gerrie, help me pack up the food. Dick? I baked my special chocolate cake, just for you."

A couple hours later, they came home. Mama Ida was sitting on my bench, enjoying the end of the day, looking at the garden, and Papa George was there, fixing one of his many rabbit traps. Dick strode over to Mama Ida with an angry look on his face. "If you wanted me to stop seeing Gerrie, all you had to do was say something and not try to poison me."

Mama Ida's face turned white. "What do you mean, Dick? I would never poison you."

Dick crossed his arms. "I'm not sure about that. Luring me into thinking you baked your chocolate cake special for me and then putting something in it to make me sick."

"I never ... Gerrie?"

By then, Gerrie stood next to Dick, carrying a container. "Mom? I'm not sure what was in that cake, but it sure tasted awful and Dick had to spit it out."

"Is the cake in there?" Mama Ida said, pointing at the container. Gerrie nodded. "Give me that."

Gerrie handed her the container. Mama Ida opened the top and took a piece with her hand. "I'll be the judge of my baking." Mama Ida took a large bite of the piece. Immediately, she spit it out.

Dick's frown first turned into a smile, then he began to laugh hysterically. "So how much salt does a great baker put in her frosting?"

Mama Ida looked up at Dick with her mouth open before speaking. "What did I do? Let me think. I was also making the potato salad at the same time. I must've grabbed the salt instead of the sugar."

"You think?" Gerrie said.

Dick continued laughing. "I forgive you, Mrs. Leinwander, but you owe me one chocolate cake ... minus the salt."

What a great sense of humor. I like Dick. I think he's a keeper, Gerrie.

***

Also during this time, I finally found out how Lucy's family, especially Kelly, were doing. Their move to Arizona was successful and the dry air was helping Kelly heal much faster; however, he still couldn't work, so he took care of the kids while Lucy worked in an office full time. Lucy wrote letters when she had a chance and kept everyone here informed, although most of the letters must have been read inside.

Hopefully, Kelly will feel good enough so maybe they can move back here. It would make Mama Ida so happy. But reading their letters outside would make me happy.

Another personal milestone for me came. I was now wide enough to see into Papa George's and Mama Ida's bedroom. Most of the time, no one was in there, unless Papa George was looking for a quiet place to nap. Usually, when they were in there, they pulled the blinds down so all I could see were shadows and light escaping from the gaps in the blinds. However, one night, before Mama Ida pulled down the blinds, she sat on the edge of the bed, with her back to me, and began to pull on the back of her hair. I knew it was long enough to put in a bun every day, but I thought it might just pass her shoulders. Her hair went all the way down her back and even partially landed on the bed.

She started to brush it with the silver hairbrush I'd noticed sitting on top of the large dresser in the room. She began to count with each stroke of the brush. As she got to sixty, it was as if she realized I was watching her. She suddenly turned around and said, "Goodness! I forgot to pull the blinds." Before she pulled it down, she looked at me and said in a joking tone, "I felt I was being watched, but it's only you, Little Ida. Pretty soon, I won't need to drop the blinds, you'll be wide enough to cover the window. But for now, down they go."

I watched in the shadows as she continued to brush her hair, counting with her, "Sixty-one, sixty-two, sixty-three …."

If Mama Ida only knew.

CHAPTER TWENTY-SIX

Dick continued to be around and pick up Gerrie to take her to her softball games or go golfing. Sometimes Betty and Bernie went with them, most of the time not. To me, it wasn't *if* Gerrie and Dick were going to marry, it was *when*.

One nice fall Saturday, the windows were open. Mama Ida and Papa George were sitting in the living room, reading the newspaper, when I saw Dick's big red Mack truck pull up. I heard him knocking on the door. Papa George left the room, and shortly, Dick came back in the room with him.

"Gerrie's not here," Mama Ida told him.

Papa George answered before Dick spoke. "I already told him that, but he still wanted to come in." Papa George motioned Dick to sit on the couch.

What's going on?

Dick said, "I know she's golfing this afternoon. I wanted to come while she wasn't here."

I saw Mama Ida put the newspaper down and Papa George scoot toward the edge of his chair.

"Well, you know Gerrie and I have been spending a lot of time together for almost a year now. I love her so much, and, well ... Mr. Leinwander, would you do me the highest honor of allowing me to ask her to marry me?"

I'm so happy. Dick doesn't look as nervous as Len did when he came to ask about marrying Pearl.

"Does Gerrie know about this?"

"Not really. I've mentioned it casually a couple of times, but she always changes the subject."

Mama Ida said, "You know how independent she is?"

"Boy, do I. I can't even do the gentlemanly thing by opening up her car door. By the time I get there, she's halfway down the sidewalk."

All three of them laughed. "Her career is very important to her also. You know that," Papa George said.

"Yes. I know that. That's why I love her so much. Her drive and independent nature fits with my personality." He then dug in his pocket and pulled out a small box. He opened it up and showed whatever it was to them.

I couldn't see what was in the box, but the sun rays hit it and it reflected beautiful colors onto the wall.

"When are you planning on asking her?"

"I want to ask in the next couple of weeks. I'm pretty sure she'll say yes, but you never knows what she's thinking." Then Dick teased, "But no picnic. I don't think I could take another one of your specialty salted chocolate cakes."

Mama Ida laughed. "No more salted cakes."

Dick always makes Mama Ida laugh whenever he's around. I sure hope Gerrie says yes.

***

The next several days seemed to keep Mama Ida and Papa George—and me—on edge. Usually, their light was out before Gerrie returned home from her dates with Dick, but now they kept their light on and, when she didn't knock on their bedroom door, but went directly upstairs, they then turned it off.

Of course, the blinds were down.

This went on for over a week. Then, one night, I heard Dick's truck pull up like usual, but instead of him getting out and opening the door for her and escorting her to the house for one last smooch, he stayed in the truck and left as soon as she slammed the truck door. I heard her knock on Mama Ida and Papa George's bedroom and soon I heard her cry.

A couple days later, Gerrie was clearing out the dead leaves and stems in the flower garden to prepare it for winter. Mama Ida came over with a hoe.

After they worked a bit, Mama Ida stood upright and, leaning against the handle of the hoe, asked, "Gerrie, why did you turn Dick down? I thought you loved him. I know he's crazy about you."

"Of course I love him. But I never really pictured myself marrying someone and staying home to cook, clean, and raise kids. I'm not saying there's anything wrong with that, and a part of me does want it, but I want more. I really love my job and I know I'd be lost without it."

"Are you sure that's what he wants you to do if you marry?"

"He says he has no problem with me working, but maybe he'll change his mind. I have other friends that happened to."

"When have you, of all people, listened to other people's issues?"

"Maybe I'm just not ready, Mom. I don't have a desire to leave home right now. I help you and Dad out with money—"

"We'll be just fine. Besides, in a few months, the upstairs apartment will be opening up and you can move in there."

"Mom, I'm just not ready."

"Okay, Gerrie. Okay." Mama Ida started hoeing again and Gerrie went to the other side of the flower bed.

She's not marrying Dick? What's wrong with her? He adores her and I know she loves him.

***

The following Sunday, the first one in October, is one of the most romantic moments I remember. The day was crisp and cloudy, so there wasn't much activity outside. Once in a while, I heard a roar of laughter seep through the closed windows while watching the family play cards.

When a break in the action occurred, Dick, who still came over, and Gerrie left the living room together. Shortly, I heard one of the doors shut and the two of them, arm in arm, walked around the corner. Dick brushed the colorful fall leaves off my bench and they sat down.

"Sure is a lovely day out here," Dick said.

"You have a funny definition of *lovely,*" Gerrie replied with a chuckle. "It's not quite forty degrees and those clouds look like they're about to give us the first snow."

"Gerrie, when I'm with you, all days are lovely."

I saw Gerrie roll her eyes and then she gently shoved Dick in the shoulder. "Really? How sappy can you get! No offense, Little Ida."

None taken, Gerrie.

"I keep forgetting I'm in love with the only unromantic woman in Appleton."

"That's not true. I'm plenty romantic." Gerrie leaned over and kissed him.

Dick got a serious look on his face. "I have something for you." He reached into his coat pocket and pulled out a small box.

"Why do you keep pushing me?"

"It's not what you think. Why don't you open it?"

Gerrie opened the box. Inside was a heart-shaped locket with a diamond set inside. "What's this?"

"I still wanted you to have the ring, so I decided to have the diamond set in the front of the locket. You will always have my heart, Geraldine Leinwander. I know you're not quite ready to leave the nest, even if the new nest is upstairs. I wouldn't want to leave, either, with your mom's cooking. Here, let me put it on you."

Gerrie pulled up her hair, while Dick unfastened the locket's latch and put it around her neck. He fastened it and briefly put his head on the back of her shoulder.

"It's beautiful, Dick," she said, fondling the delicate locket. "I can't believe you did that."

"I didn't want to return it because I bought it for you. But I have to admit, it does hurt that you don't want to marry me. We'll still see each other during bowling season and if you need a ride or a date, you can always call. But I don't think I'll come to family dinners anymore."

"But … but …," Gerrie stuttered with tears in her eyes.

"I'm sorry, Gerrie. It hurts too much. I'd appreciate it, though, if you don't say anything about this to the family, at least not until after I leave tonight. I still want one more crack at beating your mother at Sheepshead."

Gerrie smiled back at Dick while she pulled a wadded hankie out of her coat pocket and dabbed at her wet eyes. They walked arm-in-arm back toward the house.

I have a feeling I haven't seen the last of Dick LaBore.

CHAPTER TWENTY-SEVEN

Early in 1948, Bernie was still teaching in New London, so during the school year, she visited only occasionally, but she came home every summer. She was able to get a summer job in the office at Scolding Locks factory with Gerrie to make a few extra dollars while she wasn't teaching.

Gerrie was busy with her job there, running off to play sports and occasionally seeing Dick.

When is she going to realize they're meant for each other?

Pearl and Len still lived in Chicago. No children yet, but it seemed they were busy with their lives. Len became a pest exterminator and Pearl continued to work at a department store downtown. They tried to come visit at least three times a year, including Christmas.

Betty was still at the Wisconsin Power Company, slowly getting promoted along the way. She continued to play a lot of sports, but she also got a job at the YMCA, teaching sports to little kids. No particular boyfriend so far, but she seemed to go on a lot of dates and group outings.

The only major change came with Lucy and Kelly. Kelly finally got better and they decided to move to Spokane, Washington, where he knew some people who had jobs.

It seems they keep moving farther away.

All I can say is Mama Ida was *not* happy when she got that letter. She reread it angrily when Papa George came home and was trying to read the paper outside.

"George? Listen to this:

"Dear Mom and Dad: Kelly is feeling better and we decided to move the family to Spokane, Washington. He has some friends that moved there from Appleton during the war and it sounds like there's jobs in Spokane. In fact, one factory will provide us housing really cheap.

"I hate being away from home, but trying to do what's best for the family. Right now, we can only afford to live in the trailer if we move back and with the weather so harsh during the winter, coming home isn't an option, at least until we save enough money to buy a home. There's not enough room in the apartment upstairs for all of us.

"Give our love to everyone. Miss you all! Lucy"

"Ida, why are you so angry? It sounds like Kelly's getting better and they're actually going to be getting out of that trailer and into a house," Papa George said with a puzzled look on his face.

"They belong *here*. With *us*," she yelled. Then, in a soft tone that I barely heard, "I miss my grandchildren."

Papa George put the paper down, got up, and wrapped his arms around her. "I know you miss them. I miss them, too. But what are you going to do? Get them a house and jobs here?"

Once Mama Ida calmed down, she and Papa George got to their feet. As they walked toward the door, I saw Papa George take Mama Ida's hand. "I'll think of something," she said.

If I was a betting tree, I'd put all my money on Mama Ida getting them back home.

***

Mama Ida kept herself busy with her normal activities, but I noticed that Papa George was slowing down. He'd retired from the mill at the end of last year, but he developed a cough that grew worse and worse as time wore on. Whenever he came outside to putter in the yard, it always seemed that Mama Ida had some type of chore to do, too, and I noticed her eyes continually looked up from whatever she was doing to keep an eye on him.

I sure hope Papa George gets better.

One day, Papa George started tearing down the old chicken coop. They'd decided several months ago not to replace the chickens that either died or were eaten. With Lucy, Bernie, and Pearl gone, it was deemed more trouble trying to keep it going than to just buy the eggs at the store or from a neighbor. Soon, I heard Papa George coughing quite a bit and saw him stop working every few minutes. It wasn't long before Mama Ida appeared around the corner.

"George, what on earth are you doing?"

"What does it look like I'm doing?"

"You're not taking that coop down all by yourself? You were supposed to let Gerrie and Betty know so they can help."

"I'm not feeble, Ida. I can take care of this myself," Papa George replied, then began a coughing spasm.

"Listen to you cough. The doctor told you to take it easy," Mama Ida said, her hands on her hips. "Now, leave that mess there and when Gerrie and Betty get home from work, they can finish taking it down."

"But Ida ...."

"No buts, George. You promised me and the girls you were going to have them help you with the heavy work around the yard. And they can call Dick or one of their other guy friends to help."

"Those young whippersnappers won't know how to do it the right way."

"There's no problem with you supervising and telling them your way of doing things the right way." Then she walked over to Papa George and hugged him. "Please come inside. The Cubs are going to be playing soon and I have the radio all warmed up and on the right station for you."

"Ida, you worry too much. But I am a bit winded after getting the fencing down. Thanks, honey."

"I love you, George," Mama Ida said as she squeezed him again.

"Love you, too, Ida."

I wish Papa George would take it easy. But it's hard to keep such an active man down.

***

I kept growing taller and provided more shade for the bench. I wasn't quite able to see into the second floor windows, but I figured it'd only take a couple more years.

I can't wait to see where the girls spend so much of their time when they're inside.

***

Toward the end of that spring, the house on the other side of the narrow street came up for sale. Everyone who lived in our house were outside, enjoying a beautiful summer day.

"Girls, your father and I have a thought," Mama Ida started. They all stopped what they were doing and faced her.

"What about, Mom?" Betty asked.

"What would you say if we sold the cottage?"

"Sell the cottage?" they said at once, then Gerrie followed with, "Do we have to?"

"No, but with your father not feeling well lately and you girls having your own lives now, we don't think we'll be going there very often anymore. However, we were thinking of using the money to buy the house next door that just went up for sale. We figured we could make some extra income renting it out. At this point, more families are looking for places and, right now, no one wants to rent the little apartment upstairs."

"I guess that sounds like a good idea. Since the men came back from the war, there's marriages and families coming out of the woodwork," Gerrie said.

Mama Ida added, "We've seen the inside of the house and it's going to need a lot more work than we anticipated, so we're hoping you all can help get it ready in your spare time. First, though, we'll have to sell the cottage to get the money. Oh, and your father and I have an idea who we want the first tenants to be."

"Who?" Gerrie asked.

"Lucy and Kelly. If they're agreeable, how would you like it if they came home?" Mama Ida said.

"Really? That would be wonderful and worth selling the cottage for. If we want, we can always rent a cottage for a week. Much easier taking care of a home next door as opposed to one an hour away," Betty said.

Lucy, Kelly and the kids back in Appleton? And living next door? Oh, I really hope this works out.

A couple weeks later, Betty and Gerrie mentioned the cottage was sold while they walked past me on their way to softball practice.

Wow, that was fast. Now, hopefully, Lucy and the family will agree to come home.

Another week went by and the For Sale sign came down.

Please, please have them come home.

One month later, Mama Ida came out, holding a letter. Bernie, just returned home for the summer, and the other two girls were out planting the vegetables. "I have a letter from Lucy. I'm too excited to open it. Why don't you girls take a break and read this with me. Bernie, would you do the honors?"

" Dear Mom and family: Kelly and I talked it over and as much as we like it out here, we really miss you all, so we'll take you up on your offer.

" I wrote to a friend of mine who works at an insurance company in Appleton and she said they have an opening in the Claims Department. Since that's the type of work I've been doing the last couple years, it's perfect. As soon as I'm done with this letter, I'm going to get my resume mailed to them.

"With tying up loose ends here, start on our way back right after school gets done for the year. I'm hoping we'll be home before July 4th.

"Love to all and see you soon! Lucy"

"Oh, that's wonderful," Mama Ida exclaimed. "That will give us time to get that house in order. It might not be quite ready when they get here, but they can park their trailer in the yard until then. They've been living in that thing for two years now, so another month or so isn't going to hurt. I'm going to call Dick to see if he can help put in new flooring. I mean, since you two are still seeing each other." Mama Ida winked and I saw Gerrie blush.

I'm glad Dick and Gerrie are still seeing each other. Maybe, just maybe?

Over the next two months, I saw Mama Ida go across the street daily for a couple hours; the girls helped on the weekends. After a while, I saw Dick's truck stopping over occasionally, seemingly more after dinner and on the weekends, as opposed to during the normal work time the girls were gone.

I think Dick will do anything to spend time with Gerrie.

CHAPTER TWENTY-EIGHT

It was an early evening in June when I heard a car honking. Behind the car was a trailer that had luggage strapped to the top. The car had barely stopped when out popped two boys I didn't recognize at first.

You mean those two boys are Jimmy and Davey? Wow, they've grown the last two years.

Lucy got out of the front passenger side, reached back in and came out with Shari in her arms.

Shari's a little girl now. Last time she was here, she was wrapped up in blankets.

I saw Mama Ida dash across the yard, followed by Bernie, Gerrie, and Betty. They all hugged and then the boys started chasing each other around the yard. "Boys? Come here and spend time with your grandma and aunts," shouted Lucy.

"Oh, let them be, Lucy," Kelly said. "They've been cooped up in the trailer since we stopped three hours ago. I'd rather have them get their energy burned off now. Mom, do you have any lemonade made? I drank so much coffee the last week, I won't sleep for another week. Boys? Please stay in the yard and play. I don't want to look all over the neighborhood for you."

Mama Ida said, "Listen to your dad, boys. Besides, I made you all a special dinner, pancakes with currants from the bush in the back. Your grandfather's keeping an eye on the pancakes while I'm outside. Here, let me take Shari." Mama Ida groaned as she took her from Lucy. She faced Shari, touched her nose with her index finger and smiled. "My, you certainly have grown since I last saw you. Do you remember Grandma?"

Shari nodded and then asked, "Gamma, cookie ... pwease?"

Mama Ida put her down and took her hand. "Maybe after dinner, honey. Let's all go inside. Boys, you, too."

Suddenly, Jimmy and Davey stopped playing and raced into the house. Mama Ida turned to Lucy, nodded toward the boys ,and said, "I see you have your hands full. Well, we better get inside before those two eat all the pancakes!"

Those boys will sure liven things up around here.

***

Since their house wasn't quite ready yet, Lucy, Kelly, and Shari stayed in the trailer and the boys slept upstairs with their aunts. But, with the added help of Lucy and Kelly, the house was taking shape. About a month after they got here, they were able to move in and sell that cramped, well-traveled trailer. It was a good thing, too. Lucy was expecting her fourth child.

Lucy was able to get the job at the insurance company and Kelly got one at one of the large drugstores downtown. Lucy went to work early and Kelly brought the boys and Shari to our house, where Mama Ida watched them after Kelly went to work. Once Lucy was done with work, she went to her home and was there an hour before coming over and getting the kids.

Why doesn't she get the kids right away when she gets home?

It took a few weeks to find out, but one Sunday, after dinner, Lucy and Mama Ida were relaxing and watching the boys play catch in the yard. Lucy let out a big sigh. "Mom, thanks so much keeping the kids for a while after I get home. With them running around, I'm lucky if I can cook dinner, let alone get laundry and other housework done. Living in the trailer for two years, I almost forgot how draining it is taking care of a home, never mind a two story one with three kids."

"No problem. With Gerrie, Betty, and Bernie here, they take care of a lot of the housework. Besides, Shari's easy; just put some toys on the floor and she's fine. The boys? Well, we have an understanding that they can only ride their bikes around the block, and right after lunch they need to be quiet for an hour so your father can take a nap. While he's napping, or if it's raining, I'm teaching them how to play Sheepshead and rummy at the kitchen table while I'm cleaning up. They don't sit still for very long, but they do try.

"They're beginning to make friends in the neighborhood and constantly ask if they can go over to their best friend Georgie's house a couple blocks away. So far, I haven't allowed it, because I wanted to check with you first. Georgie's parents are good and I don't see any issues. Plus, they live close to the grade school and there's swings and a slide they can play on."

"I'll talk to Kelly. Maybe one evening next week we can walk down there as a family and introduce ourselves. It will be nice for them to know a couple of the kids before school starts in a few weeks."

"Well, let me know once you're okay with it. I think they try to stretch their boundaries a little once in a while. By the way, now that you mention school, did you want Shari and I to walk down there and get them after school's done for the day? I'm guessing Kelly can get them there in the mornings."

"You do so much for us already, I hated to ask."

"Nonsense. If this was a bother, I never would have asked you to move back and across the street. This is perfect for everyone."

"Thanks, Mom. You're the best," Lucy said as she hugged Mama Ida.

A couple weeks later, I saw Jimmy and Davey walk off in the direction of their friend's house. I heard Shari crying, wanting to tag along, but I saw Mama Ida holding her hand.

"I wanna go," Shari wailed and pointed toward the boys.

"Say, why don't we go into the kitchen and make a batch of sugar cookies?" Mama Ida said as she knelt down by her granddaughter.

Shari sniffled. "Fwosting, too?"

Mama Ida smiled. "Frosting, too. And you can lick the bowl all by yourself, since the boys aren't here."

Shari smiled as she wiped her nose on her sleeve. "I like when the boys aren't here."

Sugar cookie bribery will work every time.

***

The first Christmas Lucy's family was home, Papa George arranged a surprise for the kids. On Christmas Eve, the entire family gathered at our house after church. As Papa George came out to turn on my lights, a man walked up, dressed in, of all things, a Santa Claus suit.

What's he doing here?

Papa George shook his hand. "I really appreciate this, Bill. The kids will love it."

"Glad to do it, George. This old suit's been gathering dust since my kids grew up, and it's nice to get it out of the mothballs. I also found the jingle bells."

I recognize that voice. It's Mr. Radtke, Papa George's boss and friend from the mill.

Papa George smiled at him. "Give me a few minutes to get back in the house. Oh, almost forgot. The bag filled with presents is in the garage. Let me go get it."

"George, you go inside. I'll get it."

"Thanks, Bill. It's wedged behind the ladders lined up against the wall."

"Okay, see you inside."

A few minutes later, "Santa" emerged from the garage with a large sack slung over his shoulder. He slowly made his way around the house, ducking when he was close to the windows. I couldn't see him anymore, but I soon heard bells jingling, soft at first, then louder. I heard the door open and then Papa George's voice boomed, "Santa Claus! Kids, Santa is here."

I saw "Santa" walk into the room with the bag of gifts still slung over his shoulder. I saw Jimmy's, Dave's and Shari's eyes widen and their mouths open. In unison, they screamed, "Santa!"

"Ho, ho, ho," Mr. Radtke said, loud enough to seep through the cracks of the window. After that, all I could do was watch.

Kelly got up from the chair facing the window so Santa could sit down. Each child crawled up on his lap and talked with him a few minutes. Jimmy seemed to take the longest, with Santa shaking his finger at him occasionally.

Well, Jimmy is known for his pranks. I'm sure Santa's giving him a warning.

After he was done talking to each child, he reached into his bag and gave them a special present.

Mama Ida came out from the kitchen and gave Jimmy a glass of milk, and Dave and Shari each carried a small plate with cookies on one, homemade candy on the other, and I saw her point toward Santa. The kids brought the treats over to him and he quickly ate and drank his gifts. Then he brought the bag over to the tree and laid the rest of the presents around it.

I hope one day I have presents underneath me.

Papa George led Santa to the front door and said, "Bye, Santa. Thanks so much for coming tonight."

Santa scooted behind me, just out of sight of the window, which by now had three children's noses and hands pressed against it. He wiggled the string of jingle bells so they made a loud sound and then he shouted, "Ho, ho, ho. Come on, my reindeer team. We're running late. Let's get moving. Merry Christmas!"

Mr. Radtke stayed still for a while until he apparently felt the coast was clear. He then quietly went back into the garage and came out, minus the bag, hat, and beard, but with his heavy coat and returned in the direction he'd come from.

Merry Christmas, kids. I'm sure you'll remember this always.

CHAPTER TWENTY-NINE

One nice summer evening, the family decided to picnic in the yard. I always loved that; then I didn't have to strain so hard to hear what was going on.

Papa George sat at the picnic table reading the paper and Betty and Gerrie were putting the plates down when a car I didn't recognize pulled into the driveway. A very good-looking man popped up and shouted, "Hey, Betty! Is it okay to park here?"

Betty walked toward the car and answered, "Sure. No problem."

Mama Ida came out of the house with a dish full of vegetables. "Is that Willie?" One of the boys Betty had written to during the war was named Willie.

"Mrs. Leinwander, please let me carry this for you," Willie said as he raced to her side to take the dish.

"Well, aren't you polite? I sure hope this is Willie. He seems to be a keeper." Mama Ida winked at Betty.

I saw Betty blush. "Yes, Mom, this is Willie."

"Nice to meet you, Mrs. Leinwander." Willie smiled sheepishly and then shifted the dish to his left hand and shook her hand with his right.

Betty said, "Dad, this is Willie Zapp."

Papa George set the paper down and made sure his pipe sat upright on it so the lit tobacco didn't spill out. He stood up and shook Willie's hand. "Nice to meet you, Willie. I've heard so much about you from Betty."

Willie replied, "Nice to meet you, too, Mr. Leinwander. Oops, I almost forgot. Be right back." He made a dash to the passenger side of his car and pulled out a bouquet of flowers. He brought them over to Mama Ida and handed them to her. "These are for you."

"How thoughtful. I'll go get a vase."

"No, Mom. I'll get it. You and Willie get acquainted. Gerrie, come with me and let's get the rest of the food."

As they went toward the house, Papa George started smoking his pipe again, while Mama Ida and Willie joined him at the table. There was an awkward moment of silence. Mama Ida finally spoke. "Betty's told me some things about you. You met at high school?"

Once Mama Ida started the conversation, Willie said, "Yes, ma'am. She was a couple years behind me in high school, but she was in a class with me once and we became friends. We wrote to each other while I was away at war. After I got back, we kept bumping into each other because we have a lot of the same friends. Since she's such a good athlete, I thought I should start dating her. That way, when our group gets together and either bowls or golfs, she and I can be on the same team. She was always winning and I hate losing. Like they say, if you can't beat 'em, date 'em."

Papa George chimed in. "I think it's join them, not date them. But I see your point."

Mama Ida laughed and then asked, "Where do you live?"

"Across the river on the north side of town. Not far from the high school."

"What do you do for a living?"

"I'm currently working with my dad at his construction business, but I'm saving up to go to college to study architecture. I love building things."

Papa George smiled while the pipe dangled between his teeth. He must be enjoying Mama Ida grilling Willie with all these questions. He hasn't asked one question yet.

Mama Ida hesitated, then asked, "What church do you go to?"

Willie replied. "Saint Joseph's, Mrs. Leinwander."

"Oh … the Catholic Church on Lawrence Street?"

"Yes, ma'am. We go every Sunday to Mass and we're pretty devout."

"That's nice," Mama Ida said, then hollered toward the house. "Girls? Do you need any help in there?"

"No, Mom. We'll be out in a minute." I heard Gerrie's voice coming through the window.

Gerrie and Betty finally came out with the rest of the food and all five of them chatted throughout the meal. Mama Ida then brought out an apple cobbler for dessert.

"Mrs. Leinwander, this apple cobbler is delicious. It's even better than my mom's, but don't tell her I said that. I think hers is a bit too sour for my taste."

I could see Mama Ida smiling all the way across the lawn. I knew how much pride she took in her cooking. She patted Willie's arm. "Don't worry. Your secret's safe with me."

"Well, score one for you, Willie. If you want to get on my wife's good side, complimenting her cooking is the fastest way."

Later, after Willie'd left, Mama Ida was sitting on the bench by me, mending Betty's softball uniform. Betty bounced over. "Well? Isn't he wonderful?"

"Yes, he is, dear. He's handsome, funny and quite charming …."

"I feel a *but* coming."

"I'm guessing you knew he was Catholic?"

"Yeah, so?"

I was wondering the same thing.

"You do realize that will cause a major problem if you get married, don't you?"

"Why, because he's Catholic?"

"Yes, because he's Catholic. They won't recognize the marriage unless it's performed by a priest, and I'm sure it's not going to make his family happy if he marries in the Lutheran church. I haven't even mentioned raising the children."

"But, Mom, I love him. I'm sure we'll work it out."

"I'm not saying to break up with him. I'm just letting you know that if you continue down this path, it's not going to be easy, for you *or* him."

If they love each other, why is religion a problem? Betty's a good girl and this Willie seems like a perfect match for her. I don't understand.

"But otherwise, you like him?"

"Yes. Actually, I think he's a good fit for you and I think he would make you very happy."

"Thanks, Mom. I knew you'd like him."

I like him, too. He has a warm smile and seems to have a great sense of humor.

CHAPTER THIRTY

Tuesday, October 19, 1948. Papa George came out of the house on that bright, crisp fall day, walking slower than usual. I thought maybe he was moving slower because both sides of the family had helped celebrate Papa George and Mama Ida's thirty-seventh wedding anniversary the night before. The party broke up very late. He carefully surveyed the yard he'd worked on for most of his married life, watched the leaves fall from the trees, and looked at the gardens that had stopped bearing vegetables and flowers for the season. He finally came over by me and stood silently for several minutes. Now that I reached almost to the second floor of the house, I looked down at him. I noticed the constant twinkle in his eyes wasn't there now, but was replaced by tears.

He looked me up and down, forced a slight smile, and wistfully said, "Little Ida, how big you've grown these past ten years. You're already as tall as the second floor windows. My Ida made a good choice in you. I know whatever happens, you will always be here, watching over my girls." He winked at me, slowly turned away, coughing as he did more frequently the past few months, and went into the house.

I never saw Papa George again.

A couple weeks later, there was much sadness and all was quiet. The snow fell and another winter had begun.

***

The only time I saw members of the family for any length of time during that winter was when it snowed. Betty and Gerrie took turns shoveling the path between the garage and the house, but they weren't outside like usual and didn't come by me. Thanksgiving and Christmas came and went; there was a Christmas tree, but the other decorations that usually adorned the inside of the house weren't there. No one took the time to decorate outside, either, including me. No festive strings of bright lights on me this year, but that was okay. Like the rest of the family, I really didn't feel like celebrating either.

I missed Papa George. Even during the winter, he would come and check on me, especially if a lot of snow had fallen. He'd gently brush the heavy snow off my branches so they wouldn't break or bend and become deformed.

One day in January, after a large snowstorm, Betty trudged over by me after she was done shoveling. Just like her father had, she gently brushed off the heavy snow from the branches she could reach. Then she used her mittened hand to shove the snow off the bench and sat for a while.

"You know what, Little Ida? I forgot Dad used to take the snow off your branches. There's going to be a lot of things we girls will have to help Mom with, now that Dad's gone."

I saw a few tears trickle down her face. My heart broke for her. Suddenly, a strong gust of wind blew and shook the inches of snow off the branches that Betty couldn't reach, dumping all that heavy, wet snow on top of her.

She squealed at the shock of that cold snow finding its way into the crevices of her clothing. "Hey! Little Ida! What the …?" Then she started laughing.

The window next to me opened up. "Are you okay, Betty?" Mama Ida inquired. "What's all the commotion? I haven't heard you laugh so hard since before your father passed away."

"Little Ida dumped a bunch of snow on top of me, and just after I cleared her lower branches, too. Nice thank you that was, Little Ida."

"Now you know Little Ida wouldn't do that on purpose. Come inside, I have hot chocolate made."

Mama Ida's eyes followed Betty as she rounded the corner, and then she looked at me. She reached out the window. Her fingers gently touched one of my branches and then Mama Ida smiled. "Thanks, Little Ida."

Even though I didn't mean to, I'm glad I could help, Mama Ida.

***

One night in late January, I was awakened by loud noises coming from Lucy and Kelly's house. I heard a faint ringing of the telephone, then most of the lights came on in our house and I was able see Betty in boots and robe meet Kelly partway in the little street that divided the two homes and help the kids toward our house.

Mama Ida shouted, "Don't worry, Kelly. We have the kids. Just get Lucy to the hospital."

"I'll call when I know something," Kelly said.

It took a while, but eventually all the lights, except one in Mama Ida's bedroom, were off.

Lucy must be having her baby. But I thought it wasn't due for another month or so.

Nothing happened the rest of the night. In the morning, Betty took care of getting the boys to school, and Mama Ida stayed home and looked after Shari. Close to noon, while Mama Ida was making lunch,

Kelly came over. Fortunately, with the extra cooking she was doing, she'd opened one of the windows to air out the smoke all the frying was generating.

"What's going on, Kelly? The baby's early; is it okay? Is Lucy okay? I've been worried sick."

"I'm sorry, Mom. Everything happened so fast and it was just easier to come here than call. It's a boy. Lucy's doing all right, but the baby is very tiny and in an incubator. He's having some trouble breathing. They're hoping for the best, but he'll need to stay in the incubator at least a week or two before possibly coming home. It was touch and go right after he was born, we made arrangements to have him emergency baptized. We named him Glenn."

"I'm so sorry, Kelly. Can we go see Lucy?"

"Mom, I think if you come, that might cheer Lucy up. She's still quite weak, so the hospital staff wants to keep visitors to a minimum. Since we live so close, she should be able to come home in three days. Then we'll be going back and forth to the hospital to keep an eye on Glenn."

"When can I go see her? I'm really worried. Will I be able to see the baby, too?" Mama Ida asked as she hurried to prepare a plate for Kelly.

He said, "Maybe after we eat, because whatever you're cooking smells wonderful. As for the baby, you can barely see him through the window. He's in an incubator and the machine is hooked up to a lot of cords and hoses, but you can still see his face. If you could do us a favor and keep the kids overnight again, I'd appreciate it. I need to get some sleep; those chairs in the waiting room aren't very comfortable."

"Sure we can keep them another night. Actually, let's plan on the next couple of nights. If Lucy can come home, she'll need more rest and quiet if you're going to be chasing back and forth to the hospital. I'll bring over dinners, too."

"I'm so glad we came back here. We never could have handled this without you."

I'm glad you all came back, too, Kelly. We need to all take care of each other.

***

The next week was pretty quiet. Lucy came home without Glenn, but soon the kids went back to their own home and they fell into a routine. Lucy was at the hospital for several hours during the day, coming home only to get the children fed and to bed before trying to get some sleep herself. I caught bits and pieces of how they were handling everything when they picked up the kids each night. It sounded like Glenn was getting stronger, but still had a long way to go. Then the temperature outside dropped way below zero one night.

I heard the car at Kelly and Lucy's house start up just before dawn, and it backed out quite fast, making loud crunching noises in the snow. From where I was, I saw red tail lights, about a block away, racing in the direction of the hospital. Soon, I saw our lights turn on and eventually saw Betty going into their house. Since it was so early, I guessed it was to watch the kids.

They were gone a long time. Betty dropped off Shari here with Mama Ida before she took the boys to school. Then, instead of going to work, she returned home.

That's odd, she hardly ever misses work.

Around noon, I heard Kelly and Lucy come back. Looking through the windows of the house, I saw Lucy run over to ours, without a coat on, while Kelly walked slowly behind.

"Lucy, get in here before you catch pneumonia," Mama Ida shouted.

All I heard from Lucy was a sob. Then, "He's gone, Mom."

"Oh, honey, no." I heard Mama Ida sob, too. "Come inside, before we both get sick."

Where did Glenn go? Did someone take him? He didn't die, did he?

I didn't hear anything for a few days, but, with so much going on, Mama Ida forgot to pull down the shades by me, and I watched, helpless, as she cried herself to sleep every night for weeks. I knew she'd been trying to be strong for Lucy and Kelly, but with Papa George gone, I thought right now she felt lonelier now than ever.

A week later, I finally was able to hear the details of what happened to Glenn. A fresh snow had fallen, enough to cover the sidewalks and driveway. The boys were still staying at our house, but Shari'd gone back with Lucy and Kelly. Even though the boys were excited about the fresh snow to play in, they were still very subdued. Soon Betty and Gerrie came out to shovel the sidewalk and the driveway. After they were done, they walked over to me and brushed the snow off my lower branches.

"Careful, Gerrie. Little Ida has a tendency to dump snow from her top branches when you least expect it," Betty said with a very slim lilt of humor.

Very funny, Betty.

Their heads turned when they heard Lucy's house door bang shut. "What now, I wonder? Uh-oh. Lucy looks like she's going to kill someone," Gerrie exclaimed.

I thought Lucy was going into the house, but soon I saw her rounding the corner. She must have seen her sisters outside.

"Boys? Please go inside. I need to talk to your aunts."

"But, Mom, we just got out here and we're building a snow fort," Davey whined.

The look Lucy gave them made them jump up and run into the house.

If I didn't have roots, I'd run into the house, too.

"I'm afraid to ask, but what's wrong?" Betty said.

"Read this," she yelled, handing her the sheet of paper she was carrying.

"What is it?" Gerrie asked, trying to lean over Betty's shoulder to also read it.

"It looks like a bill from the hospital," Betty said. "Wait, they're charging you for delivery of the baby?"

"The gall. The nerve of them. So far, we haven't decided to sue, but if this doesn't get cleared up, and I mean today, we are going to own that hospital."

What's going on?

"They accidentally kill Glenn and then they have the nerve to send us a bill?" Lucy said while plopping onto the bench, looking the most defeated I ever saw one of Mama Ida's daughters.

I wasn't sure, but this confirms my suspicions that Glenn was dead. The hospital killed him?

Gerrie sat down next to Lucy and put her arm over Lucy's shoulder. "I guess I don't understand why you won't sue them in the first place."

"They are calling it 'an act of God' and saying they aren't responsible if anyone dies by an act of God."

"But it was their staff that was responsible. What about the other couple?" Betty asked.

"They're Catholic and refuse to. We wanted to initially, but with them not suing, plus the administrator saying we wouldn't just be suing the hospital, but the entire Catholic Church, and all their lawyers would get involved, we'd never stand a chance. Even if we would somehow win, it would take years and so much money we'd end up in the poor house. Besides, I just want Glenn back and they can't do that," Lucy finished with a raspy voice. "The only slight justice is they cancel this bill."

"Do you want one of us to go with you? I know Kelly's not home from work yet," Betty offered.

"I already called Kelly and he's able to get off work early. I also called the hospital to make sure someone from billing was still there. They don't know I work in insurance claims," Lucy said as she got to her feet.

"They aren't going to know what hit them. Good luck." Gerrie said as both she and Betty hugged their sister.

Lucy turned and started toward the house, probably to talk to Mama Ida while she waited for Kelly to show up. Betty and Gerrie sat on the recently vacated bench to rest a minute and talk.

"I still can't believe they aren't going to sue," Betty said.

"Of course, it's sort of not the hospital's fault that their furnace went out so there was no heat, but then to leave young nuns to care for the preemies, who proceed to take Glenn and the other baby out of their incubators ... that's neglect on the hospital's part. Imagine, thinking they could keep the babies warmer, but then not provide the oxygen they needed," Gerrie replied.

"Glenn would have had a better chance at home with Lucy and the rest of us taking care of him. Even if the doctors gave him under a fifty percent chance to live, he didn't even get that chance. We were prepared for him not to make it, but to have him die needlessly ...."

"I know, Betty. I'm not sure why this had to happen. Let's go inside and see if we can help Lucy. I'm starting to get cold."

"You go ahead. I'll put the shovels away," Betty said as she took the shovel out of Gerrie's hand.

"Thanks, Betty," Gerrie yelled, since she was almost rounding the corner of the house already.

I don't understand. How could a hospital make a mistake like that? I'm not going to be able to watch Glenn grow up like the rest of the kids. I wish I could go with Lucy and give them a piece of my mind, too.

CHAPTER THIRTY-ONE

After Papa George and Baby Glenn passed away, Dick started coming around the house more often. With Len and Pearl still living in Chicago, and Lucy and Kelly having their own house to take care of, Dick helped the family with some of the harder upkeep. Most of the time, he stuck around for dinner.

With Betty dating Willie, and with Dick being around a lot, it seemed natural that Gerrie included Dick when they went golfing or bowling. Whenever I saw the two men together, they were always joking and laughing and seemed to get along great.

Wouldn't it be wonderful if the girls married them? They'd be around all the time. I know Mama Ida would love that. I sure hope Gerrie changes her mind about marriage, and soon.

One day, Mama Ida was sitting on the bench crocheting a fancy doily when Gerrie came around the corner of the house. Mama Ida stopped her needlework and placed it on her lap. "Gerrie, do you have a minute? Please, come sit by me."

"What's up, Mom?"

"I know it's none of my business, but what is going on with you and Dick? He's been around an awful lot since your father died."

"Yes, he has. He's been a great help around the house."

"He sure has, but, Gerrie, I don't want him coming around anymore—"

"What do you mean? Don't you like him? I thought you did."

"Of course, I like him. In fact, I love him. But I see him mooning over you, Gerrie. It's not fair to keep him at arms' length this long. You really need to decide if you want to marry him or not. That is, if the offer is still open?"

Gerrie sighed. "Yes, it is. He brings it up occasionally. And it doesn't help that Willie teases us about it. Says he can't marry Betty until we get married."

"What's the problem?" Mama Ida asked.

"I don't know."

"Hmm. Let me ask you two questions. Do you love him?"

"Yes."

"Do you see yourself without him in your life?"

"No."

"And?"

"I'm scared, Mom. I don't cook very good and," Gerrie hesitated and finished with a soft voice, "I think I'll fail."

"Nonsense, Gerrie. That man loves you. Do you still believe, after all this time, that if he didn't know what he was getting with you, he'd still be around?"

Gerrie sat quietly for the longest time, and Mama Ida picked up her needlework.

Come on, Gerrie. You know she's right.

Finally, Gerrie said, "Thanks, Mom."

The next time I saw Dick and Gerrie, they were walking hand-in-hand, and Gerrie was wearing a sparkly new ring on her finger, along with the diamond still shimmering around her neck.

***

Yay! It's finally Gerrie and Dick's wedding day. I'm so happy for her.

Saturday, June 25, 1949 was a gorgeous day. All week, the entire family prepared the yard, brought tables into the garage, and decorated both the house and the garage with white bunting and paper bells. Mama Ida stayed up late each night, cooking and baking.

In the morning, I heard the girls upstairs, excitedly getting ready. None of the guys, not even Dick, were in sight.

He isn't backing out after all this time, is he?

Around noon, Betty and Bernie came out, wearing long dresses that looked alike, with lace yokes covering their shoulders. They wore gloves that reached up to mid-forearm, but their fingers were showing. They both carried small bouquets of flowers and there were flowers in their hair.

A man showed up and started taking pictures of the two of them. Then I saw Gerrie walk around the corner.

She looks beautiful!

She wore a long, white lace dress with a small hat on her head with a long veil attached. She also was carrying a bouquet of flowers, but it was much larger than Betty's and Bernie's. Her face was radiant. Trailing behind her were Pearl and Lucy, holding the train of Gerrie's dress to keep it from getting dirty. They wore dresses that were dark blue, with flowers on them, although their dresses didn't match exactly like Bernie's and Betty's did.

All of them stood in front of the huge, blooming bridal wreath bush a few feet opposite of me.

Why do they always take pictures in front of that bush? I always end up with the photographer's backside.

While Lucy positioned Gerrie's train, Pearl futzed with Gerrie's hair, making the curls look just right.

Soon, Mama Ida came out in a nice summer dress with a large corsage on the lapel and stood by the girls. By the time the photographer took pictures of Mama Ida, along with Gerrie and her sisters, Willie and Len had shown up in separate cars. They took a few more pictures—one even with me!—then Pearl, Mama Ida, and Bernie got into Len's car; Betty and Gerrie got into Willie's.

They were gone for a couple of hours. When they returned, honking their car horns the entire way, all the cars were decorated with bells and streamers. The last vehicle to show up was Dick's red Appleton Flooring truck. It was all decorated and with a slightly misspelled sign that read: Good By Girls! Trying To Make One - ? HAPPY!

He parked the truck, got out, and opened up the passenger side door.

Gerrie actually waited for him to do that for her.

As she got out, her hand in Dick's so he could help her, I heard him say, "Well, that's a first. You actually waited for me."

Gerrie replied, "I'm guessing that'll be the last time, too." She smiled and gave him a kiss.

What a party! The tables were laden with food and people were either drinking lemonade or beer. More pictures were taken with all the family members—of course by that blasted bridal wreath bush—and a few people brought some instruments to play music that people danced to. Later on, a huge cake was cut and a couple bottles of champagne were popped.

During the party, Willie and Betty walked hand and hand and sat on my bench. They talked about all sorts of things, held hands, and occasionally kissed.

It won't be long now before Betty's engaged. I just know it.

***

A week after the wedding, a man drove up and knocked on the door, carrying flowers. He'd been at Gerrie and Dick's wedding and was a former work friend of Papa George's. Papa George had wanted to pass on the kindness Mr. Radtke had showed him when he was first starting out in the mill and one of the young men he took under his wing was Harvey Schmidt. Once in a while, this man had come home with Papa George after work and, after supper was finished, they'd sat outside, smoking their pipes and talking.

By Mama Ida's mannerisms toward him, I'd been able to tell she didn't like him very much. She was polite, but never stuck around outside with them and, knowing her now, I could tell her smile was forced.

One night, I'd looked in the house and overheard Papa George ask her why she hadn't joined them outside.

"What do you want me to say, George? I just don't care for him."

"There must be a reason why."

"I can't put my finger on it. He sounds phony to me. Plus he seems to ogle the girls whenever he's here."

"Ida, that's just your imagination. He's a great worker and keeps to himself. I invite him over because I can tell he's lonely. You remember how well Mr. Radtke treated me when I first started. And he loves to fish and you know how much I love to talk fishing with people."

Mama Ida said, "Yes, I know. I'm sorry that I'm not interested in discussing or going fishing with you. I just have too much to do around here."

Papa George sighed. "If you want me not to ask him over anymore, I won't."

Mama Ida hadn't answered right away. Then she finally said, "He's your friend, George. If you want him to come to supper occasionally, that's fine."

I'd watched Papa George lean in and kiss Mama Ida on the check. "Thanks, sweetheart. He really is a nice guy, just takes a bit to get to know him is all."

"Whatever you say, dear."

Papa George is gone. Why is this man here? I did see him at the wedding, though. Doesn't he realize Mama Ida doesn't like him?

He rounded the corner to the opposite side of the house, so I lost sight of him, but I heard him knock.

"Just a minute." Then I heard the door open, followed by a slight pause before Mama Ida said anything else. "Well, hello, Mr. Schmidt. What are you doing here?"

"I saw these flowers and I knew I was going to be in your neighborhood, so I thought to myself, 'Who could use these pretty flowers on such a gorgeous day?' and I replied to myself, 'George's wife, I think, would love these flowers.'"

There was another pause. "They are very nice. Won't you come in?"

I know the difference between Mama Ida's polite versus her sincere voices. This definitely is her polite voice.

"I'd love a glass of lemonade or tea, if you have any made?"

"Iced tea it is."

I heard them chit-chatting about the weather, a couple stories about Papa George at work, how nice Dick and Gerrie's wedding had been, and how pleased he was at being invited. Just before he left, about ten minutes later, I heard him say, "Well, this has been wonderful. I sure miss your baked chicken casserole. I can smell it cooking now."

Is he trying to get Mama Ida to invite him to dinner?

"Well, Mr. Schmidt, since Dick and Gerrie live upstairs, I only have enough for our family, uh, especially since I didn't know you were stopping over."

"Please call me Harvey. Well, then, if you don't mind, I'll call ahead next time so you'll have enough. I think I'm available for dinner next week. Besides, I'd like to see the girls again. I didn't get to talk to them much at the wedding." I heard the door swing open. "Bye … Ida."

Oh, I don't like the sound of this.

During supper, Mama Ida told Bernie, Betty, Gerrie, and Dick about Harvey's visit.

"Mom, how could you invite him in?" Betty said incredulously.

"I didn't have much of a choice. He brought flowers and it would have been impolite to turn him away without at least a quick visit."

"Well, he gives me the creeps."

"Now, Betty, that's not a nice thing to say," Mama Ida scolded.

"I can't help it. He always looks at me funny and you should have seen how he was staring at Bernie during the wedding reception. Ick!"

"Bernie, what's your opinion? I haven't heard a peep out of you."

"If you want my honest opinion, I think he's a dink."

I heard Betty, Gerrie, and Dick howl with laughter. "Bernice Wilhelmina Fredericka Leinwander, what a thing to say!" Mama Ida replied in a shocked voice.

Boy, that's a mouthful. Is that really her full name?

"Well, he is. You wanted my honest opinion."

"I guess I better be more careful when asking you your honest opinion from now on."

"Do you want me to talk to him, Mom?" Dick volunteered once he stopped laughing.

"No. Your father told me he thought he was lonely and I'm sure he just wanted some conversation and misses your father. It was out of your father's kindness and friendship with him that I invited him to your wedding in the first place, along with several other friends of Dad's. I really don't think he'll be back."

I'm not too sure about that, Mama Ida. I don't think we've heard the last of him.

***

He didn't come the next week, but he stopped by a couple weeks later, just before the family's weekly Sunday dinner was about to start. I heard the irritation in Mama Ida's voice.

"Mr. Schmidt, what a surprise."

"Well, I was in the neighborhood and ... oh, you're about to sit down to dinner, aren't you?"

"Yes, we are." There was an awkward pause, then, "I'm sure you have other plans on a Sunday, but—"

"Oh, no. I'm not as lucky as you folks. I don't have any plans."

I think the whole neighborhood must have heard Mama Ida's sigh. "Well, in that case, would you like to stay for dinner?"

"Don't mind if I do." I heard the door slam.

All during the noon dinner, I heard Harvey's voice leading most of the conversations and sharing his opinions on every topic brought up. They played cards afterwards as usual, but the normal gaiety and shouting about who played what card wrong wasn't there. Bernie didn't even play. She came outside by me and read a book.

After eating supper and helping Mama Ida clean up, the rest of the family left. I heard Dick yawn, then say, "I think it's time for Gerrie and me to hit the hay. Mom, didn't you tell us you need to get up early tomorrow to, uh, do some bread baking?"

"You're right, Dick. I almost forgot I need to bake some bread for the Ladies Aid Bazaar coming soon. Mr. Schmidt, I'm happy you enjoyed your meals today."

"Thank you for feeding me. Next time, I promise I'll call ahead, Ida."

I then heard his car start up and drive away.

"Mom, are you sure you don't want me to talk to him?" Dick asked.

"No, I'll handle him. Besides, he said he'd call next time, so maybe he felt the awkwardness all day and realized his presence wasn't welcome."

"I highly doubt that, Mom. But I'll leave him to you," Dick said as he started up the inside stairs toward their apartment.

I agree with you, Dick. I think he'll keep coming around until you spell it out for him.

***

The following week, he came back, in the afternoon, while the rest of the family was still at work. Mama Ida was outside, watering the vegetable garden with her back to the road, so she didn't hear him walk up.

Doesn't this guy get the hint? Where's his car and why did he walk?

"Hey, Ida," Harvey called to her as he sat on my bench. "Why don't you take a load off and sit with me a while?"

Mama Ida dropped the hose and screamed, "What? Mr. Schmidt, where did you come from? I didn't hear you pull up."

Harvey patted the empty space on my bench. "Come on, Ida, sit with me a spell. But first, while you're up, would you mind getting us some lemonade? I walked all the way from my house."

Mama Ida didn't move. "Why didn't you drive? You live five miles away, if I recall."

"Don't have money for gas at the moment. I thought maybe after supper, Bernice could drive me home. She is such a number. I have no idea why she's not married yet."

Mama Ida put her hands on her hips, paused for the longest time, then strode purposefully toward him. She stood in front of him, pointed to the road, and said, "Leave. Now."

I've never seen Mama Ida so angry.

"But, Ida, why? What did I do? I'm part of the family."

"How in the world do you think you are part of my family? Please leave."

"I was invited to your family's wedding. I assumed you wanted to, um, take up relations with me."

"Relations? Like get married?"

"Well … you're widowed, I'm single. Even though you're a little older than me—"

Uh-oh. That did it.

"Get off my property. Now," Mama Ida screamed.

"Now, Ida, lower your voice. The entire neighborhood can hear you."

Mama Ida's voice quieted a little, but not much. "First off, my name is Mrs. Leinwander to you. Second, if you don't leave right this minute, I will call the police. And if you so much as step one foot on my property again, I will have you arrested for trespassing."

"How am I supposed to get home?"

"That is not my concern. And if I hear about you bothering any of my daughters, I warn you, my husband, who I'm sure now is turning over in his grave, got me a gun and taught me how to use it. Now *git*.

As Harvey took off down the hill toward the river, Mama Ida called after him, "Bernie was right. You *are* a dink!"

Bye, Harvey.

It wasn't too long before Betty appeared over the hill, coming home from work. Mama Ida was still outside, pulling weeds at a furious rate.

"Mom, was that Mr. Schmidt I saw walking away from here?"

Mama Ida continued to pull weeds.

"Mom? Mom! Is something wrong?" Betty asked more emphatically.

Mama Ida finally stopped yanking the weeds. "Everything is fine, Betty."

"You sure don't look fine. Was Mr. Schmidt here?"

"Yes."

"Mom? Did he hurt you? You're all red in the face."

I saw Mama Ida trying to calm down, but not succeeding too well. "No, honey. We just had a little, uh, disagreement, if you want to call it that."

"What about?"

"Nothing for you to worry about. But I'm positive we won't be having any further surprise visits from Mr. Schmidt. I also would appreciate you not mentioning this to your sisters or Dick. Okay?"

"Sure, Mom. I have a golf date with Willie that I need to change clothes for." Betty scanned Mama Ida one more time. "Are you sure you're okay? Willie and I can cancel our tee time and stay here."

"No, I'm fine. Really. You two have fun."

Once we heard the door to the house shut, Mama Ida came and sat on my bench. She took a couple deep breaths and said, "Oh, Little Ida. I never in a million years thought I'd have to deal with men again. I so miss George." She laughed, then said, "Imagine that man even remotely thinking I wanted to marry him. A little older than him, my eye. I can run rings around him. I sure hope I don't have to explain every detail to the girls. They'd laugh about this for years." Mama Ida laughed all the way into the house.

CHAPTER THIRTY-TWO

The spring after Dick and Gerrie's wedding was a milestone for me. This last growth spurt finally made me taller than the roof of the house, and from then on, every year I got a better view of the neighborhood.

I'd always wanted to see the places the family talked about, but since I couldn't move, I had to rely on what they said. Now I could at least begin to see the surrounding neighborhood.

Oh, look, a block away to the south is the little grocery store Mama Ida and the girls walk to, and across the street is the Sacred Heart, the Catholic Church whose bells I hear ringing every day. There's a tall building another block further south. That must be the hospital, Saint Elizabeth's, where Glenn died.

Let me look east. I see quite a few homes but, over there, a couple blocks away must be McKinley grade school where the girls sometimes play their softball games. I can't see it yet, but the girls mention cutting through the grade school grounds so the public golf course must a few further blocks.

Okay, now to the north. I can't see much, but there's a steep hill going down with lots of trees. I also see the path the girls use as a shortcut to get to the river. If the wind is just right, I can vaguely hear the rushing of the river.

Looking to the west, that must be the country club where Betty landed in the creek and twisted her ankle. Once in a while, there used to be dances and luncheons Pearl and Betty got invited to, but now only Betty goes there occasionally to golf if they're holding a tournament.

What a beautiful neighborhood. I can't wait to see how the seasons change the look of it.

***

With my new view of the neighborhood, I could keep a better eye on Jimmy and Dave. They were "a handful," as Mama Ida so kindly put it. All in all, they were good boys, but once in a while, their judgement wasn't the best. Jimmy was always thin as a reed, but Dave became muscular rather quickly and loved wrestling with his older brother. I could tell Jimmy needed all his brain power sometimes to get out of the wrestling holds Dave got him in. There were times when either Lucy or Mama Ida caught Dave being too rough and grounded him.

Jimmy, on the other hand, sometimes went along on schemes with his friends, especially Georgie, that got him in serious trouble.

When Jimmy and Georgie were ten, I heard from conversations with Georgie's mother and Mama Ida, who'd become good friends since

Georgie was over here playing with Jimmy, Dave, and Shari all the time, that Georgie's father was very ill. It wasn't too long after that I heard he passed away. Georgie's family didn't have a lot of money, especially since Georgie's father had been ill for almost a year and couldn't work, so a gravestone for him was a luxury they couldn't afford.

One day, Georgie's mother was lamenting over that fact. "I was so happy when I found out he couldn't be drafted because his knees were so bad from falling out of a tree when he was twelve, but if he was a veteran, I could get a stone for free from the government."

Mama Ida put her arm around her shoulders and said, "Why don't we have a neighborhood bake sale? I know Lucy, Mrs. Harris, Mrs. Schuman, and Mrs. Schneider would help. If each of us gets one other woman to contribute, we can raise some money. Maybe some of the ladies at your church over there at Sacred Heart would join in. If we can't hold it at Sacred Heart, we can set up some tables here in our yard. Since it's early summer, it will be easy to do it outside. It might not make quite enough money, but it will be a good start."

Georgie's mother's mouth gaped open. "You would do that for us?"

"Why not? That's what neighbors are for. And my grandchildren and your Georgie are best friends. You talk to the Ladies Aid at Sacred Heart and I'll start contacting the neighbors. Maybe we can hold it in a month or so. The boys and Shari can help make signs to put up around the neighborhood. Besides helping us, that might keep them out of trouble for at least a day." Mama Ida laughed.

Mama Ida was right. Everyone in the neighborhood pitched in. Kelly and some of the men made lures and decoys to sell along with the baked goods, and the boys and Shari made signs that I saw them pedal on their bikes as far as I could see to post. They were able to hold it at the Sacred Heart playground and, even though it was almost out of my sight range, the wind carried the sounds of laughter and someone playing songs on an accordion. Afterwards, Mama Ida and Georgie's mother came back to my bench and counted the money. They ended up making twenty-five dollars.

"This money, along with the few dollars remaining from donations at the funeral, gets me within five dollars of getting a gravestone. Thank you so much, Ida. I wouldn't have been able to get this close if it wasn't for you and your kind family."

"You're welcome. Just keep it in a safe place and, hopefully, you'll have the rest soon."

***

A couple of weeks later, it was a scorching, end of July day. Jimmy and Georgie had just gotten back from playing baseball with the other neighbor boys and settled themselves on the bench, trying to stay under the shade I was casting.

"Geez, Georgie. I am soooo hot. I'd ask Grandma for some ice cream, but we're out," Jimmy complained. "I guess I can go inside and get us some water with ice cubes or maybe just run the hose long enough for it to get cold. Then I don't have to go inside. Grandma probably has some chores for me to do and I don't want her to know I'm home just yet."

"There's ice cream and cold soda at the store over here," Georgie said.

"That costs money, which I don't have. I don't get my allowance until the end of the week. Do you?"

"No, I don't, but I have an idea where we can get some."

"Where?"

"I saw where my mom keeps the money for Dad's gravestone. There's a lot of money in that shoebox," Georgie whispered.

"You don't seriously mean taking *that* money?"

"Keep your voice down. If we only took a little, I'm sure Mom wouldn't notice."

This does not sound like a good idea.

"Are you sure about that?"

"Yeah, Mom's too busy with my little sisters to miss a couple dollars. Besides, don't you think with all the sign-making and help we did at the sale, we earned some of that?"

Jimmy, no. Why can't I tell him not to do that? I can't even throw a pine cone at him.

"Well, if you're sure, let's go. If we don't, Grandma'll be looking out the window any time and dragging me into a chore," Jimmy finally said.

They both got back on their bikes and rode toward Georgie's house. They disappeared behind some houses near where Georgie lived. A few minutes later, I saw them pedaling toward the little store a block away from our house. They went inside and soon came out, each with a double scoop ice cream cone and a bottle of pop. Just from how they acted, I could tell they knew they were doing wrong. They quickly looked around and headed behind the store.

A few days later, I again saw them coming out of the store with double scoop ice cream cones, pop, and a couple comic books. This went on every couple of days until an evening two weeks later. I saw Georgie's mother practically dragging Georgie by the arm toward Lucy and Kelly's house. Georgie's face was red and he was rubbing his behind with his free hand.

Uh-oh. I think they've been found out.

Georgie's mother marched up the front steps and knocked on the door, but then noticed the family working in the backyard. She hauled Georgie down the steps and around the corner.

"Hi, Mrs. Fuerst. Oh, hi, Georgie. I didn't see you at first. What can we do for you?" Kelly asked as Lucy joined him.

"You might want to ask Jimmy why I'm here," Georgie's mother replied.

I noticed that Jimmy was suddenly hiding on the other side of the garage.

Lucy called him, "Jimmy? Where are you? He was here just a minute ago." Lucy then shouted, "Jimmy, come here. Now."

"What have the boys been up to now?" Kelly laughed.

"This is no laughing matter," Georgie's mother said. She must have seen Jimmy peeking around the corner of the garage. "Oh, there you are, Jimmy. Do you want to tell your parents what you and Georgie have been up to?"

There was a long pause, before Kelly, in a much sterner tone, demanded, "Well, Jimmy? What have you two done?"

I couldn't hear Jimmy's response clearly, but from the reaction that happened next, he'd told his parents what I already knew.

"You what?" I heard Lucy. "We taught you better than that. Thank you for telling us, Mrs. Fuerst. How much of the money is missing?"

"Five dollars."

"Well, Jimmy will repay every cent. We'll make sure of it."

"According to Georgie, it was actually his own idea, so if Jimmy could repay his half, that would be fine."

"No. Georgie can repay what you want him to, but Jimmy will repay the entire amount. He needs to learn the lesson that we don't steal in this family. Besides, this way, you might be able to finally afford that gravestone. It might take him some time to find enough jobs, but he will repay it. Tell her you're sorry, Jimmy."

I didn't hear anything at first.

"Jimmy," Kelly shouted, "stop mumbling."

"I'm sorry I took the money. I'll pay it back, I promise," Jimmy shouted back and then I heard him stomp up the back steps into the house.

"I'm sorry this happened. It will be taken care of," Lucy said.

After that, I saw Georgie and his mom leave the house. It wasn't too long before I heard Jimmy wail and cry like I'd never heard before.

I've heard the boys talk about getting a whooping. I believe I'm hearing my first one.

The next day, I saw Jimmy coming to our house earlier than usual, occasionally rubbing his behind. I heard the door open and shut, then

Mama Ida greeted him. "Good morning, Jimmy. Why are you here so early?"

Jimmy told his grandmother everything that had happened, though Mama Ida already knew most of it from Lucy's phone call last night. Once Jimmy was done, he asked, "Do you have any extra chores I can do? Something you can give me some money for? I need to find odd jobs to pay the money back."

"Before I help you out, I want to make sure you learned a lesson. You know how hard we and all the other neighbors who gave their time worked. If those neighbors saw you and Georgie gallivanting around with pop, ice cream, and comic books, what would they think? Also, you should go to the store down the street around noon and apologize to Mr. Hermann. His store was very generous to Georgie's family by supplying the pop for the food sale."

I saw Jimmy's head hang, then he looked up with tears in his eyes. "I promise I won't do anything like that again. I knew it was wrong, but I went along with it." The tears streamed down his face.

Mama Ida looked sternly at him for a bit, then opened her arms. "Come here." Jimmy ran into his grandma's arms. "I'll tell you what. I do need some help weeding out the gardens and the rhubarb patch. Also, the back fence, where the chicken coop used to be, needs some painting. I was going to have an older boy do it, but do you think you can handle it? I was going to pay him three dollars."

"Sure I can, Grandma. I can start right away."

"Did you have breakfast? No? Well, first I'll make you a little breakfast and then you can get started. I already bought the paint. It's in the shed."

Jimmy was as good as his word. He took care of the weeds, even the ones that grew underneath me, and painted the fence a bright white. I didn't see one missed spot. Occasionally, Dave and Shari helped him, but for the most part, he did it himself. I also saw him go over to Widow Johnson's house in the next block. He mowed her lawn the rest of the summer and raked her leaves in the fall. Overhearing Mama Ida and Lucy talk, both Georgie and Jimmy made enough money by Thanksgiving, so Georgie's father finally had a gravestone.

I don't think Jimmy will be taking any more money that doesn't belong to him.

***

Len and Pearl finally moved back to Appleton from Chicago. They bought a small house on the other side of town, according to the bits and pieces I heard from the family and when they came for Sunday dinners. One time, Lucy took Shari with her to Pearl's house for a visit. After they got back, Shari found Mama Ida working on her crocheting on my bench.

"Well, how was your visit to your Aunt Pearl's house?" Mama Ida asked as she moved over enough for Shari to sit down. "I've seen it, but I'd like to know what you thought of it."

"Her house is so sophisticated."

"Sophisticated? My, that's sure a fancy word for a little girl. You know what? You're absolutely right. I never thought of it like that. But what did you think was so sophisticated about it?"

"It looked like it came out of one of the ladies' magazines that my mom reads. It was so pretty and fancy. The living room was red and it was decorated with a Japanese … oh, shoot. I can't think of the word she said. It started with an M."

Mama Ida jumped in. "Are you thinking of the word 'motif?'"

"Yeah, Grandma. That's the word, motif. I was afraid to touch anything, and Mom told me not to, but Aunt Pearl said I could, if I was really careful, which I was. There were statues of people dressed in kimonos, which I just learned about in school, and a few large fans with paintings on them spread out and attached to the wall. I don't think I'll ever forget it. Have you ever seen anything like that?"

"No, dear. I'm afraid I haven't. The only place I've ever seen anything like it is at your Aunt Pearl's. Do you think her house is pretty?"

"Oh, yes, Grandma. It's beautiful."

Leave it to Pearl to decorate her house all fancy. I wish I could see it.

CHAPTER THIRTY-THREE

Betty and Willie did everything together. He was over almost every day, usually picking her up and then they either played golf or bowled together. On the weekends, Betty was dressed up and they went to dances. If the weather was nice, when they got back from wherever they'd gone, they sat on my bench, holding hands and kissing. If the weather was bad, I watched through the window and saw them turn on the radio and dance together. They listened to Frank Sinatra, Doris Day, Bing Crosby, The Andrews Sisters, and Perry Como.

When they were around, Jimmy and Dave teased them. Willie would stop dancing, chase after the boys, and when he caught one, he lifted his prey up in the air and dangled him upside down by their ankles. They'd laugh and scream until Betty finally told him to stop, but never without tickling them first to exact her revenge. Everyone in the family seemed to love Willie.

I love Willie, too. They are so in love and perfect for each other. I sure hope he proposes soon.

***

Mama Ida was working in the garden in late April when Willie stopped by.

"Betty's still at work, Willie."

"I know. I came to talk to you."

I saw the seriousness of Willie's face. Mama Ida looked at him for a second and then said, "Would you like a glass of lemonade? I just made some this morning. I know I sure would."

"That would be swell, Mrs. Leinwander."

As Mama Ida went into the house, Willie sat on the bench and turned toward me. "Little Ida? Betty tells me she talks to you occasionally. Maybe if I quick practice with you, I won't be so nervous to talk to her mom."

My curiosity was piqued.

"Mrs. Leinwander? I love Betty and I want to ask you for her hand in marriage. I realize you have concerns regarding the differences in our religions, but we'll work them out. I'm not sure if I'm ready to convert, but I'm seriously thinking about it," Willie said nervously.

A voice answered behind him. "Of course you have my permission, Willie. I'm sure you will provide for Betty wonderfully and, better yet, have the patience to deal with her. I know her career and sports are very important to her. I do still have some concerns over religion, but I just can't imagine Betty marrying anyone else, but you, so I'll get over it."

Willie blushed, jumped up off the bench, and turned to face Mama Ida. He then looked back toward me. "Little Ida, maybe give me a warning next time," he teased, laughing. He turned back to Mama Ida once again. "Thank you, Mrs. Leinwander. I know we'll be very happy. I can't wait to ask Betty."

A few days later, when Willie and Betty came home from their date, they both went inside. Usually, Willie escorted Betty to the door, they'd talk a bit, and he'd leave. Not this time. I saw the kitchen light turn on, but a minute later, I heard the record player in the living room softly play *For Sentimental Reasons:*
Please give your loving heart to me
And say we'll never part

They began to dance. Every once in a while, when Betty turned a certain way, the glow from the kitchen caught a glint of something on Betty's finger.

It wasn't long before I saw the light of Mama Ida's bedside lamp turn on. Through the shade, I noticed her shadow go towards the door, but it stopped there. I heard her soft chuckle and the shadow returned to the bed and the light snapped off.

Betty must have said yes.

***

One late July day, they were in the yard playing croquet when suddenly, Willie doubled over. "Geez, my stomach really hurts!"

Betty asked worriedly, "Did it just start?"

"No, it started yesterday, after I got hit in the gut with that line drive at my baseball game, but the pain went away. Now I can't hardly stand up straight."

"Let's get you to Saint Elizabeth's. I'll drive you there."

"No, I think I just must have pulled something. It will go away, I'm sure." As he straightened up, his face went pale and he started to fall. Betty grabbed him and helped him to the bench.

"Wait here. I'll get Bernie to help me."

They got Willie into the car and sped the couple blocks to the hospital. I could just see to the entrance of the emergency parking lot two blocks away. Now I had to wait like the rest of the family.

Bernie drove back without Betty about an hour later, but it wasn't until early evening that I saw Betty walking home from the hospital.

Bernie and Gerrie were outside. "How's Willie? What's wrong?"

It took Betty a moment to speak. Her eyes were red. "The doctor says he has appendicitis. They took him into surgery. I called his parents and I waited with them until the surgery was done. The doctor's not sure if he's going to make it because his appendix burst," Betty said as she choked back tears. "He did survive the surgery. But since I'm not officially family yet, I couldn't see him. They said I might be able to see him tomorrow, if he's doing better."

"I'll go with you and if they won't let you see him, I'll make them. You're practically husband and wife," Gerrie said defiantly.

"I will, too," Bernie piped in. "By the way, Mom's got dinner on the table. Let's go inside and let her know what's going on."

"I'm not very hungry. I think I'll sit out here for a bit," Betty said.

Betty sat by me quietly.

Why can't I have arms to hug her?

I saw her hands folded in prayer and her lips whispering. About a half hour later, Mama Ida came out and sat next to Betty.

"He's strong, Betty. Young and strong. I will pray, too. Please come in and eat a little something. I made a sandwich that's for you. It will help you sleep."

"Okay, Mom," Betty said, and they both went into the house.

He needs to be fine, for Betty's sake.

***

The next day, Betty, Gerrie, and Bernie went to the hospital. About two hours later, they came back, giggling. "Willie must be doing better?" Mama Ida asked while she was doing her mending, sitting on my bench.

"Yep, he seems to be. But that's not why we're laughing," Bernie said. "Gerrie put on the performance of a lifetime."

Betty interjected, "You see, the nurses still wouldn't let me see Willie. His parents weren't there, so there wasn't anyone to vouch for me. Gerrie *promised* me she would get me in to see Willie …."

"So," Bernie continued, "Gerrie wrapped her arms around her stomach and started moaning in pain. She was so convincing, Betty at first didn't move. Finally, Gerrie slyly motioned at Betty with her hand to get moving."

"I guess I had the nurse convinced I was sick. She sat me down, took my temperature and blood pressure. It took me almost an hour to talk myself *out* of the hospital." Gerrie said.

"But Gerrie got me in to see Willie. The nurse guarding the intensive care area was so busy with her, she never did notice me sneak into his room."

Mama Ida laughed, but then turned toward Betty. "Well, how *is* he?"

Betty's face turned somber. "He's pretty weak and still looking quite pale, but he did have his sense of humor. Told me I wasn't getting out of our wedding that easily. I'm still worried, but I feel a little better since I got to see him. He has all those tubes sticking in him. I gave him a kiss and told him I'd see him tomorrow after work."

***

The next day is another one of those dates I will always remember: July 24, 1950.

A car I didn't recognize parked on the street next to the house late that afternoon. A couple, who looked around Mama Ida's age, got out and knocked on the door. I heard Mama Ida say, "Hello, Mr. and Mrs. Zapp. Please come in. I hope Willie's doing—" I didn't hear anything else. By then, they were in the house. It was a coolish day, so the windows were shut.

Soon, I saw Betty determinedly coming up the hill. I'd overheard her this morning say she was going to the hospital as soon as she was done with work. Since the house was a direct line in her path from work to the hospital, she was striding across the lawn when she saw the strange car parked on the street. She stopped, changed direction, and hurried into the house. I didn't hear anything for a few moments, then Betty screamed, "No, no, no. You're lying! I'm going to the hospital now to see him!"

Then I heard the door slam and Betty started running toward the hospital.

"Betty, Betty, come back," Mama Ida yelled from the opened doorway. "Bernie? Go after Betty."

A few minutes later, Willie's parents left. Betty, with Bernie's arm around her, came home about an hour later. I saw Mama Ida open her arms and Betty fell into them, sobbing. "Why, Mom, why? Why Willie? Why my love? I can't … just can't …."

The door closed.

I found out later that Willie died from a massive infection the burst appendix caused inside him.

Betty cried for months. I wished there was something, anything I could do for her. The only thing I could do was just be here for her.

CHAPTER THIRTY-FOUR

The summer Willie died, Bernie came home from New London, just like she'd done the last few years. This time, she looked different. She looked sadder somehow and always seemed lost in thought. She puttered around the garden with Mama Ida, worked at her summer job, and played softball with her sisters, the same as every summer since she started teaching, but there didn't seem any of the usual joy. It was like she was just going through the motions.

One Saturday afternoon, after Betty and Gerrie left to go golfing, Bernie sat on my bench, writing a letter.

Mama Ida came out with two glasses of iced tea. "How come you didn't go golfing? I know your sisters enjoy spending as much time as they can with you while you're home."

"I didn't feel like it. I'm trying to figure out what I'm going to do with this offer to teach at the East Fork Apache Reservation in Arizona next fall."

"Are you really thinking of taking it?" Mama Ida asked in a worried tone.

"Actually, yes. I can't go back to New London. It hurts too much. So far, this is the only offer to go somewhere different."

What happened?

"You can't always run from your problems."

"Mom, I loved him so much. He took me out to dinner several times, sat with me in church, and talked about future plans. He even kissed me a few times." I saw Bernie blush. "Really good kisses. But then, *she* came back in town and the following week, he told me he still loved her and was going to ask her to marry him."

Who is this she? And who is this guy that hurt my beloved Bernice?

Bernie continued, "I can't keep seeing them around town and at church. The town is too small. Even the couple weeks before school let out, I bumped into the two of them together holding hands three times. I just couldn't bear it." Bernie started to cry.

Mama Ida reached over and pulled her heartbroken second-oldest daughter toward her and hugged her tight for several minutes as Bernie sobbed into her bosom. She then gently pulled her up and looked her in the eye. "I've never seen you so upset. You've always been my easy daughter: studious, happy, kind, and beautiful. I hate seeing you like this. Maybe a fresh start somewhere totally different might be good for you, even though it's on the other side of the country."

"I just couldn't bring it up with everything that Betty's gone through. My problem isn't as big as hers. Having my boyfriend break up with me is one thing, but having Willie die is much worse," Bernie said as she finally caught her breath.

"Yes, it's tragic that Willie died, but your problems are just as important to me as Betty's. All my daughters' problems are important to me."

"Thanks, Mom. You know, I've been in all my friends' weddings. I guess I'm destined to never marry. Like they say, 'Always a bridesmaid, never a bride.'"

"Well, honey ...," Mama Ida looked like she was searching for words to comfort her, "maybe there isn't any one man for you. But you have dozens of children a year that you teach how to read and write. That is such a gift. You're still young. Things may change."

"Maybe. So you don't mind if I accept the position? I really want to take it, but I didn't know how to tell you."

"Of course I don't mind." Mama Ida paused. "Okay, I do mind. You realize, there will be no trips home for Christmas or Easter while you're down there. It's too far away and expensive to come home for a week of school break, like you were able to do from New London and college. It'll be the first time you'll miss being here. Also, it's an Indian Reservation out west, so that whole world will be very different from what you're used to and still a little on the wild side. The people, climate, language, everything."

"I'm actually excited, Mom. Maybe this is what I'm supposed to do with my life. I'm not going to know unless I try."

"I'll see if Gerrie or Betty can take some vacation when you leave to help you settle in."

"Mom, I need to do this myself. They can visit—in fact, I'd like you to visit, too, but I'd rather move out there on my own. If I end up never getting married, I'll have to figure these things out for myself. I haven't done a bad job so far, have I?"

"No, honey. You've gone back and forth from Oshkosh, New London, and even Minnesota. I just thought—meant—you might like the company. That trip will take you a few days."

I think Mama Ida wants to help Bernie without it feeling like she's helping.

"Uh-huh. Sure you did." Bernie finally smiled. "I know what you were up to. I love you."

"I love you, too."

I'm used to you being gone, Bernie, but sounds like this reservation place is really far away. You better write lots of letters.

Bernie taught in Arizona for one school year. From the few letters Mama Ida read out loud, she loved it—the mountains, the desert, the temperature, but mostly her students. Sometimes she included drawings the children made of their homes, the mountains, and animals. However, she also wrote how much she missed everyone here and I could tell from the words Mama Ida read that she was homesick.

One late April day, Mama Ida brought the mail over to my bench to look through it.

"Hey, Little Ida, there's a postcard from Bernie." She flipped the card to the back, read it silently, and smiled. Then she turned and looked at me with tears in her eyes and said, "Oh, Little Ida, listen to this. 'Saint Paul offered me a first grade teaching position at the school for next year. I'm coming home!' Did you hear that, Little Ida? Our Bernice is coming home. I need to let Betty, Gerrie and Dick know when they get home from work."

Whoopee! Bernie's coming home.

There were finally a few changes in the family dynamic, as well. Lucy and Kelly's youngest daughter, Carol, was born in 1950, then, early February in 1951, Pearl and Len were finally blessed with a son, Leonard Jr., or Little Lenny, as he was affectionately called. In late April, 1952, Mama Ida welcomed another grandchild to the family. Gerrie and Dick's daughter, Janette, nicknamed Jan, was born. The house was full of babies and toddlers.

MY MATURE YEARS

CHAPTER THIRTY-FVE

For Christmas in 1953, the girls chipped in and bought Mama Ida her first television set. I was able to peek at it through the window. Besides the sounds like what came from their radio, it also showed pictures.

There were some shows I recognized from the radio, *The Milton Berle Show, The Jack Benny Show,* and *You Bet Your Life,* a game show hosted by Groucho Marx. And there were a couple new shows Mama Ida and the girls watched: *I Love Lucy, The Jackie Gleason Show,* and *Arthur Godfrey's Talent Scouts.* The only problem was, even if it was nice outside, if it was a show Mama Ida or one of the girls liked, they stayed inside instead of coming out by me.

How can I be less important to visit with than a stupid, noisy box?

During this same time, whenever the family was together, they talked about a man in Washington who came from Appleton, Senator Joseph McCarthy. According to them, he was stirring up a lot of controversy in the nation's capital about people in high positions possibly being Communists. Once the war ended, the new enemy seemed to be Communists or "The Reds," as the men in the family called them. I certainly didn't know anything about these "Reds," but it sounded like this guy from Appleton was hell bent on stopping them. At first, everyone seemed to be behind him.

As time went on, the family's thoughts on him began to change. Some of them thought he was still trying to do what was best for the country, but others thought he was going overboard, especially when he started going after Hollywood actors and high ranking officers in the military.

One show that they all watched and talked about during this time was called *See It Now,* hosted by the famous reporter, Edward R. Murrow. I remember him broadcasting news from the war, and if it was something he said, people tended to believe and trust him.

On March 9th, Mama Ida and the girls huddled around the television set, watching this show. It was still very cold out, so I could only watch through the window, but the host seemed to be going into detail about Joseph McCarthy. It must have been very convincing because a few weeks later, all they talked about when they came outside to start cleaning up the yard from the usual winter clutter was about this show.

"I'm almost embarrassed he's from Wisconsin, let alone Appleton,"

Betty said.

"Murrow sure had some pretty damning evidence against him. McCarthy's been saying a lot of things about other people without having anything to back it up, and Murrow seemed to prove that, at least to me," Bernie added.

"Well, he didn't help himself when he came on the show a couple weeks later to rebut what Murrow said," Mama Ida chimed in as she bent down to pick up some of the limbs that had fallen during the winter.

"I know. Murrow's so smart and he used Joe's words against him," Betty said, puffs of steam coming from her mouth as she started raking some of the old leaves that gathered in the bare flower bed.

"I guess we'll all know what's going on in a couple weeks. They're going to televise the Communist hearings. Mom, you'll have to give us a rundown of what happens while we work. Hopefully, it will still be going on when I'm off from school during spring break," Bernie said as she helped Betty with raking the leaves into a pile.

"Oh, I'm quite sure of it. Wouldn't be surprised if it lasted into the summer. Don't forget, these are all politicians who love to hear themselves talk."

That's a long time. These guys must have a lot to say.

Mama Ida laughed as she tossed the twigs she'd picked up onto the leaf pile. "You girls finish up, I'll start on dinner."

Mama Ida was right. The hearings went from April to June and dominated all the news on both the television and the radio, plus it seemed to always be a topic of discussion during the weekly family Sunday dinners.

Eventually, I learned that Senator McCarthy was banned from speaking on the Senate floor by the rest of his peers. He didn't run for re-election, and died a few years later.

***

The summer of 1955 was the oddest, quietest summer I ever experienced. I didn't hear any of the usual noises of children playing in the neighborhood. Even though Shari, Carol and Lenny were dropped off each morning and picked up around suppertime, they, along with Jan, rarely came outside to play, and always stayed in their yard. I also noticed that, most of the time, the windows were shut.

What's going on? Did everyone get allergic to being outside for the summer?

Even the adults didn't stay outside too long, but there were still chores that needed to be done: mowing the grass, tending to the vegetable gardens, and so on. Fortunately, once a week, Mama Ida came outside and sat with me, quietly doing one of her many projects.

One week, as Mama Ida was doing her knitting, I saw Bernie pull the lawnmower out of the garage. She started mowing, but once she got by Mama Ida, she stopped and took a small break.

"Mom, you shouldn't be out here this long."

"Bernie, I'm not going to be shut inside all summer. Once a week for a half hour shouldn't hurt anyone," Mama Ida replied.

"No one knows how fast the disease will travel."

What disease? Can trees get it?

"Bernie, I'm old. It seems to only really affect little kids to young adults. I figure, if it's my time, it's my time. I'm not going to waste the entire summer inside. Besides, if I don't escape out here once in a while, Jan, Lenny, Shari, and Carol are going to drive me nuts. I'm glad the three of them come over each day during the summer and play with Jan to keep her entertained, but sometimes it's a bit much."

Bernie sighed. "I heard Sally Wollersheim down the street got a mild case of it. At least, that's what the doctors think. I bumped into her mother at the grocery store."

"I hadn't heard. I'll make an apple tart to bring over," Mama Ida said.

"I sure hope this polio epidemic is over soon so school can start. But I'm not looking forward to the beginning of school this year. Last thing those kids will want to do is sit still and spend more time inside. I foresee a lot of gym classes on my schedule."

"About Sally, did they have to put her in an iron lung?" Mama Ida asked.

"No, they caught it in time. Sounds like she probably will have a limp the rest of her life, but that's better than being paralyzed or dying.

Isn't this the same disease President Roosevelt had? He couldn't walk and needed a wheelchair.

" I heard a doctor invented a vaccine that the kids will get at school, once it starts. It's supposed to stop them from getting it," Bernie said. "Well, I better get back to mowing. If your grandchildren see us out here chit-chatting, they'll insist on coming outside and it's hard enough keeping them entertained. At least Shari's old enough to help us keep them amused. I think she might grow up to be a schoolteacher," Bernie said proudly.

"As soon as I get this row finished on the blanket, I'll go inside. Then I'll start working on that tart."

It sounds like trees can't get polio. No wonder all the children in the neighborhood are staying inside this summer. I feel so bad for them. It's been a nice summer.

Not too long after this conversation, a woman knocked on the door that led up to Dick and Gerrie's apartment. It was Jan's best friend, Mamie's, mother. I heard someone come down the steps and Gerrie answered the door. "Why, Margaret, what brings you here? Why don't you come in?"

"I can't stay long. Could we sit on the bench and talk for just a minute?" she said nervously.

"Sure. Dick?" Gerrie yelled. "I'm boiling potatoes on the stove, would you turn it down?"

"Okay," I heard him respond faintly. "I'll take care of it."

Both women walked down the four steps that led to the door and then sat on my bench. As custom with this disease, they sat as far apart as they could.

"Gerrie, I wanted to let you know that Mamie has polio. She was diagnosed this morning."

"Oh, no. How is she?"

"The doctor thinks they caught it early, like Sally down the road, but she's very sick." Margaret said, looking down at her hands.

"Is there anything we can do for you?"

"Just pray, but that's not why I'm here. The doctor also told me to contact any parents of children that came in contact with Mamie in the last three weeks."

Gerrie looked puzzled. "Why are you telling me ... wait, did Jan sneak over there?"

"Not exactly. I saw through the window both girls were playing in their own yards, but with our backyards kitty corner from each other, both Mamie and Jan eventually wandered over and began playing dolls with each other. They both knew where each of their yards ended and obeyed our orders to stay in their own, but they still touched each other and exchanged dolls. Once I saw them together, I ran out of the house and got Mamie away from her and told Jan to go back to the porch. It was about a week ago. Since Mamie or Jan weren't experiencing any symptoms, I didn't think much of it at the time, but I know I should have called you. I'd feel just awful if ...." Margaret, with her head in her hands, seemed not to be able to complete her thought.

"Yeah, you probably should have told me then, but I might have reacted the same way, if I were you. Thanks for telling us right away. We'll get her tested tomorrow and I'll keep her from her cousins until we find out. I'll let you know the results as soon as I can," Gerrie said in a worried tone.

"Thanks, Gerrie. I sure hope Jan's tests come back normal."

"Me, too, Margaret. Me, too," Gerrie replied as she hurried back up the steps.

Jan has to be okay. I don't know what I'll do if she was sick with this.

I saw Jan playing upstairs for a week, but overhearing conversations between Gerrie and Dick, then with the rest of the family, her tests came back negative. Even though the remainder of the summer and fall were difficult, the epidemic was finally over and people returned to their normal lives.

I'm glad it's over, too. It was an awfully lonely and worrisome summer for me.

CHAPTER THIRTY-SIX

That next summer, Lucy and Kelly built a brand new house outside of the city limits on the west side, so Len and Pearl moved into their vacated house. Lucy's children came over occasionally, but mostly for Sunday dinners and other special occasions. Both Jimmy and Dave were older and had jobs, so I hardly saw them anymore. Shari was old enough to take care of Carol for a few hours.

I sure miss them and their energy. One good thing about us trees, we don't move away when we get older.

But Mama Ida and Jan grew very close, since Gerrie and Dick still lived in the upstairs apartment. Once Jan was old enough, Gerrie returned to work at The Brady Company and Mama Ida took care of Jan during the day. They sat outside when it was nice; Jan played in a small sandbox Dick built for her near my bench and Mama Ida brought out whatever portable chores she could do outside. Jan loved playing cowboys and Indians, tag, and hide-and-seek with her cousins, especially Lenny, since he was right next door.

Sometimes, though, Jan cuddled up with Mama Ida, her head on her grandmother's lap, and Mama Ida told her stories about her mom and aunts when they were young.

I love listening, too. I get to learn more about my girls from before I came. They weren't children anymore when I first got to know them.

One day, Jan and Mama Ida were outside, enjoying a rare, hot day in the spring.

"Grandma? I'm thirsty. Can I have a glass of lemonade?"

"*May* I have a glass of lemonade, *please?*" Mama Ida gently corrected.

Jan smiled. "Grandma, may I have a glass of lemonade, please?"

"Yes, you may. But you will need to sit on the bench and drink it. Your plastic glass is upstairs and I don't want to climb the stairs to get it right now. You will need to drink out of a grown-up glass."

"I promise, Grandma."

Mama Ida returned shortly with two glasses of lemonade. Jan sat quietly on the bench and sipped hers. Mama Ida must have been thirstier; hers was gone in two gulps.

"Okay, Jan. Sit here and finish your lemonade while I go pull some weeds out of the garden." Jan nodded as Mama Ida got up and headed across the crooked sidewalk to the vegetable garden.

At first, Jan sat, obediently sipping her drink. Then a beautiful butterfly floated right next to her.

Jan loves butterflies.

She jumped up, drink in hand. As she began running down the crooked sidewalk, her toe caught on one of the raised edges and she fell. Fortunately, she landed on the grass, but the glass of lemonade wasn't so fortunate.

Crash. Then sobbing from Jan.

Mama Ida got up and rushed over to her. "Are you okay? Here, stand up and let me look you over. Doesn't look like any broken bones. I think you're fine, just some grass stains."

Jan continued to cry. Mama Ida and Jan carefully stepped over the broken glass, and the lone trickle of leftover lemonade soon escaped into the sidewalk's crevices and evaporated away.

"Sit down. Why are you crying? Does something hurt?" Mama Ida asked worriedly as she hugged her inconsolable granddaughter.

"Grandma, I broke your rule. I left the bench and broke the glass. I'm sorry."

"Why did you get up?"

"There was a beautiful butterfly going to the flowers and I wanted to see it. I forgot about the glass. I'm sorry." Jan looked up at Mama Ida, tears still flooding her eyes.

"Accidents happen. I know you didn't mean to. If I saw a beautiful butterfly today, I'm sure I would have totally forgotten about the glass, too. Did I ever tell you the story about Aunt Betty dropping the milk bottle?"

"No. You mean Aunt Betty broke something?"

"Yep, and it was much bigger and more important than a glass of lemonade."

"What happened?"

"Well, a long time ago, I gave your mom and Aunt Betty a dime and sent them to the little store a couple blocks away to buy milk. That was a lot of money back then."

"How old were they?"

"Let me think. I believe your mom was twelve and Aunt Betty was almost six. Aunt Betty begged and begged to go with your mom. I finally let her go, but I specifically told them that your mom needed to carry both bottles. Somehow, on the way back, Aunt Betty talked your mom into letting her carry one of them. Your mom said Aunt Betty promised to hold it with both hands. However, just like you did, Aunt Betty wasn't watching where she was stepping and tripped on the sidewalk. She didn't fall, but she lost the grip on it and *splat*," Mama Ida interrupted the story by clapping her hands, "there went the bottle. Milk and all."

"What happened then?"

"Of course, I didn't know what had happened yet. Suddenly, the screen door opened and slammed shut. Aunt Betty was wailing and tearing up the stairs at lightning speed. I saw your mom walking across the street, so I waited for her to come inside—with one bottle of milk. I asked, 'What's wrong with Betty? And where's the other one?' Of course, your mom told me that Aunt Betty refused to come home with her unless she carried one of them.

"Your mom said, 'I'm sorry, Mom, but I couldn't help it. She just wouldn't budge unless I gave her one. She insisted she was old enough to carry it and promised to use both hands. She was concentrating so hard, she forgot about the large crack in the sidewalk and tripped. She didn't fall all the way, but the bottle slipped while she tried to keep her balance and it broke. Mom, she really was doing a good job,' your mom finished saying, trying to keep your Aunt Betty out of trouble."

"What did you do to Aunt Betty? Did you spank her?"

"No, I didn't spank her. I let her cry alone for a few minutes, then I went upstairs and sat on her bed. I couldn't see her, but I certainly heard her. I finally got on my hands and knees and lifted the comforter. She was hiding under the bed. Well, to completely hide, besides not being able to be seen - you shouldn't make a noise either. Remember that, Jan, when playing hide and seek with your cousins."

Jan giggled.

I giggled, too. Usually, Jan hid behind me in the corner, between the steps and the house wall, quiet as a mouse, when hiding from her cousins.

"I asked your Aunt Betty, 'What are you doing crying under the bed?'

"She said, 'I ... I. .. b-b-br-oke the milk bot-bot-tle. I'm sorry, Mama. I didn't listen.'

"'Well, according to your sister, you were doing a good job, so good, you forgot about the huge crack in the sidewalk. Next time, if you promise to be just as careful, but knowing now to watch for the cracks, you can go and get a bottle of milk on your own.'

"Jan, your Aunt Betty crawled out from under the bed with the biggest smile on her pudgy little face. She hugged me and I told her to go downstairs and help your Aunt Pearl, who was setting the table for dinner at the time."

"You didn't punish her?"

"No. I think she punished herself enough for the not listening to me part. The rest was an accident, right?" Mama Ida looked at Jan with one eyebrow raised. "Something like what happened just now?"

Jan was silent for a minute. "Yes, just like now. Thanks, Grandma. I love you!"

Mama Ida squeezed Jan. "I love you, too." Mama Ida stood up and grabbed Jan's hand. "Let's go inside the house, get you cleaned up, and I'll come back out and pick up the glass. I don't want you to cut yourself."

"Are you going to tell Mama?"

"Only if you tell her. Otherwise, it will be our secret."

I won't tell either, Jan.

***

A few days later, Jan plunked herself next to Mama Ida while she was doing some crocheting. "Grandma? Tell me another story about my mom."

Mama Ida looked at her sternly.

"*Please* tell me another story about my mom?"

A smile crossed Mama Ida's face. "Let me think. Well, there was one day, similar to this one, beautiful and warm, just perfect to play outside. Her cousins were visiting from New York and she planned to play outside all day. But when she woke up in the morning, her face was flushed and when I touched her forehead, she felt really hot—"

"What does *flushed* mean?"

"It means her face was really, really pink."

"Oh."

"Anyway, I called the doctor. Your mom kept telling me she felt fine and didn't want the doctor. I think she was about ten years old. While waiting for the doctor, she insisted on going downstairs to get a glass of water. The doctor showed up about fifteen minutes later, checked her out and took her temperature. He told me, even though she was flushed, she didn't have a fever. I thought it was odd, but he was the doctor. She bounded out of her bed before either the doctor or I could change our minds and was outside in no time flat. I was curious how your mom managed to not have a fever. I looked under the pillow, the sheets, and finally under the bed. Tucked in, just behind her favorite doll on the floor, was the glass of water she'd gotten before the doctor came. There was some water in it, but not much. Most of the glass contained ice cubes. Your mother, your very smart mother, sucked on ice cubes right before the doctor came upstairs, so her mouth was very cold when he put the thermometer in her mouth. A couple days later, when she still wasn't feeling well, I called the doctor back, but I kept a close eye on her that time. The doctor said she had pneumonia."

Jan giggled. "I'll have to try that sometime."

Mama Ida touched Jan gently on the nose with her index finger. "Oh, no, you don't, young lady. Between your mom and me, we know that trick now!"

Boy, Gerrie was clever at such a young age. Jan's learning a lot, having Mama Ida around.

***

I do remember one late, warm, spring day, while Mama Ida was looking after Jan, the sky suddenly began to grow very dark. Jan was playing in her sandbox and Mama Ida, as usual, was taking care of the vegetable garden. I saw she was so involved with pulling weeds she didn't notice the ominous clouds forming quickly in the west.

"Grandma, look at the pretty black clouds," Jan said as she pointed to the sky.

Mama Ida finally looked to see what Jan was pointing at. Almost simultaneously, sirens began to sound. Mama Ida quickly headed toward the sandbox where Jan continued to play.

"Quick, Jan, grab my hand. We need to go into the basement."

"Grandma, is everything okay? My doll is in the house."

"She'll be fine where she's at. We're closest to the outside door to the basement. We better get down there before it starts to rain."

It was like the clouds heard Mama Ida. They opened up and it began to pour. The wind whipped around the yard so fast several young trees began to bend dangerously. A neighbor's garbage can from across the street took off into the air and almost hit Mama Ida. Jan started to cry.

"We've got to go to the cellar, now." Mama Ida turned toward me briefly. "Stay strong, Little Ida." Then she grabbed Jan's hand and they disappeared down the crooked, uneven concrete steps that led to the basement door.

I'll be fine. Just take care of you two.

I heard the door shut.

The storm came quickly. I'd lived through storms before, but this one was the worst ever. When the tree on the other side of the yard snapped in half, I really became worried. The birds and squirrels that called my branches home huddled in their nests. I clung onto their nests with my branches as tight as I could and brought them close together to help keep them as dry as possible. Throughout the neighborhood, I heard several other trees snap. Loose newspapers and garbage flew past me faster than any bird I'd ever observed. My trunk bent and twisted in directions it wasn't not meant to, but luckily, with the wonderful care the family gave me while I was growing, I was strong from the highest twig to the lowest root.

I huddled with my tiny companions, protecting them the best I could. At one point, I saw Jan's sandbox pail get picked up by the wind;

it danced in the air for a minute before blowing close to me. I dared to stretch out one of my branches and was able to snag it when it passed by.

I sure hope they look up and find it for Jan.

As fast as the storm came, it left—with a mess in its wake. Leaves and branches cluttered the yard and the bird feeders were nowhere to be found. One of the new trees, a maple Dick had planted near me, had fallen and blocked the outside stairs going to the apartment. I also saw a couple trees down at the neighbors. Soon, I heard the basement door creak open and, slowly, Mama Ida and Jan emerged. Once they got to the top of the steps, Jan hurried over to her sandbox. "Grandma, my pail is gone!"

"I'm sorry, honey. The wind must have blown it somewhere."

"Look, Grandma, a tree is down." Jan pointed towards me, since the maple tree was in the same direction.

I briefly saw a panicked look on Mama Ida's face as she glanced at me first. Then her eyes followed Jan's finger to the maple tree on the ground. "That's too bad. Your dad planted that for me a few years ago. Once he comes home, guess he'll have some work to do. Why don't you come with me and let's check Little Ida over, okay?"

They walked to me and, while Mama Ida checked my lower branches, Jan went to the other side of me and looked up. "Grandma, come here. Little Ida saved my pail!"

Mama Ida strode over and stood next to Jan. "Sure enough, she certainly did. I guess the very first thing on your daddy's list is getting the ladder out to rescue your pail. Now, let's get into the house. I'm quite sure there's something to clean up in there, since I didn't get a chance to close the windows."

As they turned to go into the house, Jan reached up and softly touched one of my branches. "Thank you, Little Ida, for saving my pail and I'm glad you're okay."

Any little thing I can do for you, Jan.

CHAPTER THIRTY-SEVEN

After Willie died, Betty concentrated mostly on her job. Eventually, the spring came back in her step and she did have a couple boyfriends, but mostly she did things with Bernie, Gerrie, or one of her friends from work. She went on trips, like to Sun Valley to ski, or she took the train to Milwaukee to watch the Braves play. Sometimes one of her sisters or friends went with her. I could tell she was lonely, but I think she was resigned to the fact that Willie had been the one and that was it for her.

One day in the early fall of 1956, Betty walked home from work slower than usual. Her head was down, and she was concentrating on kicking a stone along the sidewalk by the house, seemingly deep in thought. "What's up with you?" I heard Mama Ida say as she gradually unfolded herself from the middle of the garden and arched her back. "I don't think I've ever seen you walk so slowly, especially *from* work."

"Well, you remember Pete, the salesman that stops in my office weekly from Chicago? He and his wife came for supper at our house about three months ago after we golfed? He told me he has a friend back in Elmhurst, Illinois, who's perfect for me—or at least his wife, Louise, thinks he is. He's a couple years younger than me, a plumber, and he loves sports. They want to bring him up here next weekend to go bowling and have dinner. Not sure if I want them to do that. What do you think?"

"Well, I think it's a good idea, as long as you're comfortable with it. Of course, if he's a gentleman, he will insist on stopping by and introduce himself. You know how old-fashioned I am about these things, especially since your father passed away."

"You do realize I just turned thirty-three years old a couple weeks ago. But the plan is that they'll stop and pick me up here, so I'll make sure you get to meet him," Betty said.

"Only advice I can give you is always be yourself. You're very smart and, unlike a lot of women, you're extremely good at sports. Don't ever lose on purpose or pretend to be dumb just to impress someone. Maybe that attracts some men, but those aren't the men you want to marry, because you'd be absolutely miserable. He needs to love you for who you are."

"Mom," Betty replied, exasperated, "you know it's not in me to lose on purpose. And it's just one blind date. It's not like I'm going to marry him or anything."

A year later, on July 19, Betty married Jim Cutler, plumber and friend of a salesman, at her church.

***

Hang on, it wasn't as easy as it sounded. Jim lived about two hundred miles away, near Chicago. Betty read and wrote several letters to him, many of them while seated on my bench. He came once a month, in his convertible, and picked her up from work on a Friday. He stayed first at a local hotel, then, after Gerrie and Dick bought their own home a couple months later, with them. Dick and Jim became great friends. The four of them spent a lot of time together, golfed, bowled, and the three of them taught Jim to curl. It wasn't long before Jim proposed.

Betty accepted, but not without a few issues. Even though they'd dated about a year, since he lived so far away, most of their courtship had been through letters and occasional telephone calls. From the conversations I overheard between Mama Ida, Betty, and her sisters, they had their doubts if he was right for her.

One nice fall afternoon, all the girls, along with Mama Ida, were sitting together in the living room with the windows wide open, and started to question Betty on her relationship.

"Jim is charming, really charming, but you've only seen him a few weekends over the year, since he lives so far away," Lucy said. "How well do you really know him?"

Is Betty going to move to where Jim lives?

"Are you worried you're not going to meet someone?" Pearl asked.

"I'm doing fine without a husband," Bernice added.

"You know I love Jim, and so does Dick, but your engagement seems rather fast. If this is because you miss Willie …." Gerrie tentatively ventured to say.

"This has nothing to do with Willie," Betty said angrily. "Of course I miss him, but he's gone and I have to get on with my life."

Mama Ida took a deep breath. "Do you really love him, Betty? If you're not sure, you're also uprooting him from a good job down in Chicago to take a chance on living up here. That's going to be a hard adjustment for him."

Whew. Jim is going to move here.

"Yes, Mom. I love him. I know he's rough around the edges, but he grew up poor in southern Illinois and he's finally feeling like he's getting somewhere in life. I do feel like we're a good fit. There's one issue, though, we need to resolve before I walk down any aisle with him."

I could tell Betty's sisters and Mama Ida were taken aback by that statement. No one said a word until finally Gerrie's curiosity must have gotten the best of her.

"Okay, that came out of the blue. What's the problem?"

"Well, last night, we were talking on the phone and he wanted to know when I was going to quit my job at the power company, now that we're engaged," Betty said.

"Quit your job? Doesn't he understand how much you love your job?" Gerrie asked, and not in a nice tone, either. It appeared the rest of them were content to have Gerrie lead this conversation, so they sat back and just listened.

"I told him that, but he said he didn't want his wife working."

"But—"

Betty held her hand up and Gerrie stopped abruptly. "For now, it's fine. I reminded him that when he moves up here, he won't be able to get a job right away anyway, so I will have to support us until he can pass his Wisconsin plumbers license. However, this conversation will continue the next time he comes up." Then Betty looked at everyone, especially Gerrie. "When he does come, not a word from any of you. I will handle this. Promise?"

"Fine. You handle this," Gerrie retorted, but then continued with a sisterly voice. "But you know we'll back you up, whatever you decide."

"Besides, we'll be living upstairs, so you can keep an eye on us," Betty said.

Betty and Jim are living here? I'm so happy.

***

The next weekend, Jim came for a visit. They'd just gotten back from golfing and sat on the bench, drinking some iced tea.

"What's up with Gerrie? She hardly spoke two words to me all afternoon. We both know that's not like her. Come to think of it, your mom and Bernie were a bit standoffish this weekend, too."

"We need to talk about something before we continue with the wedding plans," Betty answered, looking at her hands.

Jim looked crestfallen. "What? Did I do something wrong?"

"Not exactly, but I'm really not happy with our last phone conversation."

Jim looked thoughtful for a moment. "I don't remember us having an argument. Let me think ... wait, does this have to do with you working?"

"Yes, it does. Even when you do pass your Wisconsin plumbing license test, I am not quitting my job. I love it too much."

"But I want to take care of you, and by then, I'll have the means to be making a good living. Then you can stay home and take care of the kids."

Betty shook her head. "First off, what am I going to do all day? Since we'll be living upstairs at first, there's not much to clean, and Mom will want us to eat with her and Bernie most of the time. I'll be so bored and it's just not ... me. Secondly, what if we don't have any children? I'll be almost thirty-five years old by the time we get married and there's a possibility I might not be able to have children anymore. Then what will I do? Jim, my career is very important to me and it's part of who I am. I just wouldn't be the same person and I feel I might resent you if you insisted."

Jim sat silent for a moment. "Okay, say you don't quit your job, but if you do become pregnant?"

"Well, if that happens, I will have to quit my job because it's a power company rule once they find out I'm pregnant. But not until then," Betty said with a firmness that I'd never heard from her before.

"Well, I was brought up thinking women wanted to stay home and be taken care of and that's just how things are done back where I'm from. What attracted me to you was your independence, strength, and intelligence, and I certainly don't want to interfere with that. You're right, you keep working as long as you want. What about your job at the YMCA?"

"I already planned on quitting once we're married. I mostly did that a couple evenings to fill some of my spare time, and the extra pay wasn't bad, but now I guess I need to be around those evenings that aren't league nights," Betty said, then asked more seriously, "You don't have a problem with my golf and bowling leagues?"

"Nope. I plan on joining one or two men's leagues once I move here permanently. Hopefully, we can squeeze in a couple's league, too."

"I think that can be arranged."

I think Jim is finally understanding not only Betty, but the rest of the family.

***

The next day, before Jim went back to Chicago, he and Dick were outside, working in the garden. Dick asked Jim, "So, I heard you and Betty had your first tiff."

Jim shrugged and replied, "Did you already know about Betty's issue regarding her working after we got married? If you knew about it, well, that explains why Gerrie seemed a little put off by me all weekend. How come you didn't warn me?"

"It's yours and Betty's business and Betty specifically told Gerrie not to interfere. She didn't tell me all the details, but she's been fit to be tied after talking with Betty last week. They may have their occasional disagreements, but upset one of them, you upset all five ... plus Mama Ida," Dick said with an amused look on his face. "You'll learn."

"I guess I just didn't realize how important working was for Betty. Thought I was doing her a favor."

"No. They want to be busy, and, to them, being busy is having a career. Even Lucy. Though she started out being at home since she married right out of high school, she now is continuing to move up as an executive at the insurance company she works for, and not as a secretary."

"You're right and Betty's right. What if we end up not having any kids, since we're both older? She's been at the power company almost twenty years and we really could use the money to save for a house." Jim stood upright, walked and shook Dick's hand. "I need to start driving home. Thanks for listening. Now I know who to go to for advice."

Dick gently slapped Jim's back with his free hand. "Don't mention it. I'm always here. Be safe driving home."

I think Betty will keep him on his toes. Welcome to the family, Jim.

CHAPTER THIRTY-EIGHT

On April 9, 1957, after Betty and Jim got engaged, Betty came running up the hill and burst into the house. "Is it here yet? Is the newspaper here yet?"

"I think I heard the paper boy slam it against the door, why?" Mama Ida replied.

"The article about Gerrie and me is supposed to be in there today. In the sports section. I can't wait for you all to read it, especially Jim."

"Well, while you go and get it, why don't I fix us some coffee. We'll sit in the living room," Mama Ida said in her most calming voice.

A few weeks ago, Betty and Gerrie had come home from bowling with big news, big enough for Gerrie to come inside, too, and for them to wake Mama Ida up in her bedroom.

"Mom, wake up. We have some news for you," Betty said.

"Is anything wrong? What's Gerrie doing here? Did one of you bowl a three hundred?" Mama Ida asked in a sleepy tone.

"No, nothing's wrong," Gerrie said. "One of the newspaper's sports reporters was at the alleys tonight and wants to do a story on us. He also wants to talk to you."

"Me? What would I have to say to a reporter, especially one who does sports?"

"I don't know, Mom. He said he's looking for a special interest story on women playing sports and someone at the paper told him about us," Betty said.

I saw Gerrie nudge Betty. "It's probably because your name's been in the newspaper a lot these past couple of years with your bowling," Gerrie said jokingly.

"Maybe. I *have* been bowling and golfing well these past couple of years. All that extra practice with you, Dick and Jim," Betty said.

"Well, since it's not happening tonight and both of you work tomorrow morning, you'll need your beauty rest in case there's any pictures for this. Plus, Gerrie still needs to drive home," Mama Ida said as she rolled over to go back to sleep.

"I have to run upstairs and tell Bernie," Betty said as Gerrie left.

I can't wait to hear this news article. I sure hope they read it out loud so I know what it says.

Suddenly, the phone rang and interrupted my memories.

"Hello. Leinwander residence," I heard Mama Ida answer. "Oh, hi, Gerrie. No, we haven't read it yet. Betty was just going outside to get the paper ... you'd better get here soon. You know how impatient Betty can be. I'll make sure Jan's ready. See you in a half hour, Gerrie."

"Betty, Gerrie called," Mama Ida said as Betty returned with the newspaper. " She'd like us to wait until she gets here since she has to pick up Jan."

"I know. I promised her I would." Betty huffed. "I guess while I'm waiting, I have enough time to change out of my work clothes and get ready to go teach at the Y. Is Bernie home from school yet?"

"Not yet. Hopefully, she'll get here in time to hear the article, too."

"I hope she's not mad. I included her name when the reporter interviewed us, but he said it's only supposed to be about the two of us. I guess more than two athletic females in a family is more than they can handle."

Mama Ida sighed. "Well, hopefully, with women like you and Gerrie, you'll help change that opinion."

Fifteen minutes later, Betty was back downstairs, eating a sandwich and sitting on the couch with Jan, waiting for the rest of them to show up. A couple minutes later, I saw Gerrie's car pull up and both she and Bernie got out.

"Thanks for picking me up, Gerrie. I want to be here when you both read the article for the first time," Bernie said.

"No problem. Glad I thought of it on my way here. The school is only a couple blocks out of my way, so I thought I'd check and see if you were still there," Gerrie said.

Betty shouted, "Well, it's about time you got here. I have to leave in fifteen minutes."

"Yeah, yeah. I know. Your life is so rough, Betty," Gerrie said as she entered the living room, followed by Bernie and then Mama Ida.

Betty pulled out the sports section. Through the window, I saw a nice picture of the two of them, standing next to each other, with their beautiful smiles. "I can't read it," Betty said. "My hands are shaking."

Bernie got up from where she was sitting and took the paper from her. "Nice picture of you two. Here, why don't I read it?

"Sisters Dominate Roll of Top Bowling Scores. That's the headline. Betty Leinwander, Gerrie LaBore also curl frequently, enjoy other sports." Then Bernie giggled. "Like Ida Cantor, Eddie's wife, Appleton's Mrs. Ida Leinwander has five daughters and no sons. But it's unlikely that any pair of Mrs. Cantor's offspring can approach the athletic record of two of Mrs. Leinwander's gals.

"This reporter must be taking a creative writing class. I certainly wasn't taught to write that way in the one journalism class I took in college."

"Bernie, keep reading," Gerrie and Betty said in unison.

"Fine." Bernie read out loud their bowling records and a mention of their curling exploits that were in the article. "Oh, here's a cute mention about Jan. The birth of Gerrie's child didn't hamper her athletic activities too much. Jan was born in April,' Betty relates, so Gerrie just missed one week of bowling and several weeks of golf."

Bernie continued reading more of their bowling records listed in the article. "Oh, I didn't realize this, Betty. It says here, the last two seasons, Betty has owned the highest women's average in the city. Although all 1956-57 returns aren't up to date, she's near the top again."

I saw Betty's smile all the way across the room.

Oh, Betty, I'm so proud of you. Both of you.

"It continues," Bernie said. "Tuesday is one of the evenings that she is teaching gym at the Y. And that's after putting in a full day's work as a supervisory clerk at the Wisconsin Michigan Power Company."

Bernie then read more statistics both girls performed over the last couple of years. "It now goes on to mention your golfing. Oh ...."

Gerrie, who had been quiet most of this time, said, "What is it, Bernie? You're not done yet, are you?"

"Yes, I want to hear you read the end of it," Mama Ida said.

I heard Bernie's voice go softer. "Betty, who is a bit heavier and has darker hair than her spectacled sister, is the better golfer of the two, averaging about forty-five for nine holes. When asked about her average, Gerrie replies, Just say I play golf too."

Bernie stopped. I saw both Betty's and Gerrie's faces become crestfallen. There was a short, awkward silence broken by Mama Ida. "Is there any more, Bernie?"

"There's three small paragraphs more. A great interest in athletics on the part of their parents got the girls started in sports. Mrs. Leinwander is their number one fan, Betty says. Both Betty and Gerrie are concerned about the lack of organized competition for women athletes in the area. Outside of bowling and curling leagues, there aren't many opportunities for gals with athletic ability and a yen for competition."

Bernie finished up. "Their favorite sports? Gerrie prefers team sports - she liked softball best of all. Betty enjoys all of them, each one in its season.

"That's it."

After a short pause, Mama Ida spoke. "I think it was a fine article. I'm so proud of all of you."

"Mom, I can't believe it. Why did he go into those physical descriptions? And he didn't mention I was getting married in a few months. He made me sound so ... so mannish and ugly. I was so proud of that article, but now ...."

"Well, Betty. You, of all people, know how certain men have limited ideas about girls who are athletic and they need to justify it to themselves. I hope someday that will change—and I think you and your sisters are going to be some of the reasons it will."

Gerrie added, "I agree with Mom. Men are still getting used to the idea that women have the same competitiveness in both sports and work. It's just going to take time. Ten years ago, the newspaper wouldn't have even thought about doing an article like this. I know you're hurt, but all of your family and friends who know and love you won't even give these comments any thought. Jan? We need to get going. I know your father's making dinner and I don't want to be late. It's meatloaf night."

That was such a great article. Why did that reporter have to write that and hurt the two of them? Sometimes humans can be so dumb and hurtful without even knowing it.

***

July 19, 1957, didn't come soon enough for me.
It's Betty's and Jim's wedding day.
Betty, Bernie, and Mama Ida all got dressed at the house. From what I'd overheard, Jim was staying at Gerrie and Dick's house and was getting ready there. I was able to peek into the second floor where I saw Mama Ida help Betty put on her veil and Betty help Mama Ida with her corsage.

"I sure wish your father was still alive to walk you down the aisle, Betty. Are you sure you don't want me to walk with you?" Mama Ida asked.

"No, you go down ahead of me and sit in the front pew. I won't be walking by myself. Dad will be with me in spirit."

Bernie, dressed in a beautiful pink dress, helped Betty with her train down the stairs.

Soon, they came outside and walked over to my side of the house.
Oh, no. Not that blasted bridal wreath bush again!
They each took turns taking pictures with Betty because someone had to hold the camera.

"I wish we would have booked the photographer to come here first, since the wedding reception is at the American Legion and not here," Betty said, sighing.

"I'm sorry, dear. Money's a bit tight and I think you'd rather have nice pictures at the church and reception. For the extra thirty dollars, we all felt it wasn't worth the cost."

"I know. Mom? Before we leave, would you take a picture of me with Little Ida? She always seems to get the short end of the stick because we take pictures with the bridal wreath bush and she always gets our backsides."

Betty, thank you for thinking of me on your big day.

Betty stood in front of me while Bernie fixed her dress and made sure her bouquet looked good. I straightened my trunk and stretched out my branches as much as I could. I wanted this to be *the* best picture. Then, right before Mama Ida snapped the picture, Betty smiled and glanced up at me.

"Now, that's going to be a great picture," Bernie said, then looked down at her watch. "Hey, we better get going, Betty, or you'll be late for your own wedding."

Take that, stupid bridal wreath bush!

Earlier, Betty had parked her car on the street by the back door, so they were able to get into the car quickly and drive away.

The next time I see Betty, she will be Mrs. Jimmie Cutler.

CHAPTER THIRTY-NINE

In the fall of 1959, the family decided to have a big party to celebrate Dick's hunting luck. He'd shot so many pheasants and grouse that no one had any more room in their freezers. They chose Sunday, November 8, as the big day.

It was a beautiful fall day. The entire clan was home. I heard plans for Thanksgiving and Christmas being talked about as dinner was served. By early afternoon, everyone was full from eating bird, and I could hear the shuffling of the playing cards, which meant a Sheepshead game was breaking out. Laughter, groaning, good-natured ribbing, poker chips bouncing on the table, children giggling and chasing about were just some of the sounds. But I heard Mama Ida's laughter over all of them. As always, she was happiest when she had her brood around her.

During a break in their card game, Betty and Mama Ida came outside for what I assumed was a breath of fresh air.

"It's such a beautiful day out, isn't it, Betty? Let's sit by Little Ida for a minute."

"Mom, I wanted to ask you something. Now that Jim's settled in a great plumbing job, we can afford a family, but nothing's happening yet. You don't think, just because I played, and still play, a lot of sports, that's stopping me from having children?"

"That's an old wives' tale, Betty. You're a little older than most women trying for their first one and I think God doesn't think it's time for you yet. Everything will come in time. Besides, you'll want to have your own home," Mama Ida said.

"That was the other thing I wanted to talk about. Jim and I've discussed it, and, in the spring, we're going to start looking for houses. There's a lot being built on the west side, just outside of Appleton, near where Lucy and Kelly bought," Betty said.

"Hopefully, you'll find something. You have time," Mama Ida said.

"I just don't want it to be too long. I want you around to help."

"Betty, I have no plans on going anywhere. I know I'll get a chance to dote on your babies, just like I did the others."

Just then, in the distance, I heard a yell. "Betty, Mama! Where are you? Everyone's back at the table. Are you guys playing or not?"

Mama Ida patted her youngest daughter on the knee. "Well, Betty? Time to teach those young'uns a lesson in cards."

I agree with Mama Ida, Betty. Just be patient. There's all the time in the world.

***

After a light supper of leftovers and one more round of cards, everyone went home.

I saw Betty and Jim go upstairs to their apartment. About an hour later, I heard Bernie start shouting for help. Lights turned back on, and soon an ambulance, with sirens blaring, roared up to the other side of the house. It seemed like forever, but, eventually, the ambulance drove away, quietly and slowly toward the hospital.

***

I lost my beloved Mama Ida.
There was almost unbearable sadness. All was quiet. The snow fell and another winter began.

***

The winter after Mama Ida died was a harsh one. Lots of snow and below zero weather. Jim took over all the shoveling duties, but he didn't have time to chat with me. He *did* occasionally brush the snow off my lower limbs.   All the families came to the homestead for Easter and, since it was a nice day, the girls and their husbands were outside, looking over the yard.

I hope they start talking about Mama Ida. I want to know what happened. Now that it's getting nicer out, I'm going to miss her so much. And, with Mama Ida gone, will they sell the house? It sounded before like Betty and Jim were going to be moving out, so will Bernie be able to stay here?

"Our offer on the house on Timmers Lane was accepted this week, so we can't buy this one. But we won't move until the end of June," Jim said to the group. "That will give Bernie time to decide if she wants to stay or have us help fix it up to get ready to sell."

"Do you still want to live here, Bernie?" Pearl asked. "It's a big house, so if you'd rather sell it, we understand."

"No, I can't imagine living anywhere else. The house really isn't that big. I won't use the two bedrooms upstairs for anything but storage and I'll find someone to rent the apartment when Betty and Jim leave. Once that income is coming in, I'll be able to pay all of you for your portion of the house," Bernie replied as she sat on my bench.

"We're not concerned about the money. You don't owe us anything," Dick said. "We just want to make sure you don't feel you have to stay."

"No, Dick. Really, I want to stay. I love the yard and I worked so hard to come back here after all the different places I lived. Besides, who will look out for Little Ida if I move?"

Whew, I'm so happy Bernie is going to stay. This way, I'll see everyone occasionally.

"I'm still not over the shock of Mom dying from a heart attack," Betty said. "We had such a good conversation that afternoon and, to me, she looked fine. I guess if she had to go, that would be the way to do it. She won at cards, we were all there, and she was so happy. I'm glad you've decided to stay here, Bernie. I was dreading the thought of losing Little Ida, too."

You and me both, Betty.

***

Once Betty and Jim moved to their new home, Bernie rented the apartment to a young couple for a couple years, then each of Lucy's sons and their new wives, first Jimmy, then Dave. It worked out great because it was a little cheaper for them so they could save for houses of their own. After Dave left, Bernie was able to rent the apartment to one of the teachers at her school.

Shari went to DMLC, just like Bernie had. She became a teacher, married a man who was also a teacher, and they moved to Michigan. Carol also married and started a family of her own. All four of Lucy's children became busy with their own lives and families and were only able to come around at Christmas.

But I really missed Mama Ida. The girls all had their own homes, so Sunday dinners rotated between them, which meant the families only came over when it was Bernie's turn once a month or so. The routine was the same, but the extra laughter from Mama Ida was always missing.

CHAPTER 40

Late in 1961 and early 1962, a few changes in the family came along. After a Sunday dinner in early November 1961, Betty, Gerrie, and Bernie came outside to enjoy one of the last nice days of fall. Bernie and Betty sat on my bench, while Gerrie examined the remnants of the flower garden nearby.

"Betty, are you sure? Have you gone to the doctor yet?" Bernie asked.

"I went on Friday. The doctor confirmed it," Betty said.

Gerrie said, "How are you feeling?"

Betty replied, "A little sick to my stomach, but other than that, really good."

Gerrie smiled. "See, all that worry was for nothing."

Nothing? It sounds like my Betty is sick.

"Does the doctor know when you're due?" Bernie inquired.

Due? Is she …?

"He feels the baby should come late May, probably before Memorial Day. Actually, close to your birthday, Bernie."

She is! Oh, Betty is pregnant! Did you hear that, Mama Ida?

"That's great. Mom would have been so happy." Bernie said.

Betty's face saddened. "I know."

All three of them were quiet for a minute, but then Gerrie broke the silence. "Well, I guess I should start finding a bowling sub for you. How about after the first of the year? Oh, and what about our golf league?"

Betty thought for a minute. "The golf league? I think I'm going to skip it this year. By the time I'll be ready to golf, half the season will be over. Besides, I'm sure it'll take me some time to learn the ropes of taking care of the baby. You all had me to practice on growing up. Bowling? Yeah, a sub when you mentioned is probably best. The doctor said I'm fine to continue activities as long as I feel up to it, at least until I'm six months along. However, this took so long to happen, Jim and I don't want to take too many chances, so after the first of January sounds great. Besides," Betty said with a grin, "the baby weight will begin to throw off my balance and my average might go down."

They all laughed. "Well, we wouldn't want *that* to happen," Gerrie said.

"Also, I'm hoping to keep the pregnancy a secret until March. This is the only time I'm grateful that I'm heavier. I can hide the pregnancy until then. After that, I plan on leaving my job—or hopefully they let me retire. I have my twenty years in now."

"Nothing like retiring at the age of thirty-eight," Gerrie said, but then continued on a more serious note, "By the way, while we're gabbing together, I want you to know I'm applying for a new job."

"Where at?" Bernie asked.

"Actually, City Hall. There's an opening for deputy treasurer of the city and it sounds interesting."

"How come?" Betty asked

"I think I've gotten as far as I can at the Brady Company, and if I'm going to do something different, I better do it now before I get too old. I'm going to be forty-five in a couple of months, you know."

Both Betty and Bernie laughed. Betty said, "You? Too old? You still move around too fast for age to catch you."

They laughed harder as they started back into the house.

Oh, how badly Mama Ida would want to be here for this. I'm so proud of them!

***

In late May of 1962, Betty came and sat by me. Since I hadn't been trimmed in a couple of years, my branches reached past the back of the bench and brushed up against her back. "Little Ida, I have someone to introduce to you." I looked over her shoulder and saw her cradling a small baby. "This is Karen Beth, Kari for short. This is my daughter. Wouldn't Mom have been so happy?" She started to cry.

Fortunately, a gentle wind came at that perfect moment, and my overgrown limbs caressed Betty's back. *Yes, Betty. Mama Ida would have loved that little one.*

"I always feel Mom here. Thanks for the comfort, Little Ida. I knew I'd feel better coming by you. Next Sunday is her baptism day. Gerrie and Dick will be her godparents."

I'm so glad I still can help you feel better and make you smile.

Betty continued, "Say, when I get back inside, I better ask Jim to move the bench forward a bit. You're getting so big. I'd do it, but, you see, I have my hands full at the moment. Also, I should check with Bernie to see if she needs help paying to have a tree company come in and trim you. Spruce you up a bit, so to speak," Betty said, then her face saddened. "Dad and Mom wouldn't be happy with us if we didn't keep you looking nice."

I can't wait for this little one to grow old enough to play in the yard just like you used to, Betty.

Three years later, Kari got a sister named Kathy Lee, eventually nicknamed Casey because Kathy couldn't pronounce her th's. Once

Casey got to be four years old, Betty and Jim joined a couple's golfing league with Gerrie and Dick. So every Friday, they packed the girls up and brought them over here for Bernie to watch. They usually played in the yard for a while, then Bernie hustled them into the car with a bunch of lilacs and a bag of old breadcrumbs.

I wondered why on earth she took those things, but eventually, I found out they went to the cemetery where Mama Ida and Papa George were buried to put flowers on their graves and then the three of them fed the ducks in the cemetery's pond.

I wish I could go and visit their graves. Bernie? Maybe take some of my pine cones. The graveyard is way over on the other side of town and there's no way I can ever see it.

***

A few years after Casey was born, Jim bought the plumbing business he was working at and Betty started to run the office for him. During the summer, Bernie took care of the kids while all three were off from school. They ran and biked around the house, just like their mom and aunts used to do, or they helped Bernie with the gardens. They loved picking up the pine cones I dropped so Bernie could use them as arts and crafts projects for her first graders.

Bernie, being Bernie, also took them to the library once a week and both girls always came back with a pile of books. And even now, every Friday, since Betty and Jim continued to golf in their couples' league, Bernie and the girls kept their ritual of going to the cemetery in the late afternoon to put fresh flowers on Mama Ida's and Papa George's graves and to feed the ducks.

I feel so bad for Kari and Casey. They never got to know Papa George's quiet ways or feel all the hugs and kisses from Mama Ida.

CHAPTER FORTY-ONE

Oh, I almost forgot about Tinkerbell. After Mama Ida passed away, Bernie decided to get a cat she named Tinkerbell. Bernie gave her roaming privileges outside. She never strayed too far from our yard; she was a smart Siamese and knew where meals and a warm bed were. She loved to sun on my bench but gave me a look of disdain if I created a shadow and she needed to move. She also had a few litters of kittens who all played around my bench before they were big enough to be given away to friends. Tinkerbell was a great mouser who loved to rummage in the flowers that surrounded my base, seeking them out. She reigned over the yard, just like the queen Siamese she was.

When Tinkerbell was about three years old, new neighbors moved into the house next door, including their large, over fifty-pound Airedale terrier. He decided our yard was part of his domain and came over constantly, much to Bernie's and my dismay. He loved to dig and I was constantly worried he would dig around my roots. He also used our yard as his personal toilet and his owners never came over to clean up after him. Whenever Bernie saw him sniffing around the yard, she'd either yell out the window or come outside and chase him away. It was pretty comical-looking, but I appreciated it nonetheless.

It wasn't long before the Airedale chose the wrong day to check out Tinkerbell's sacred yard. She was lying on the bench, with one of my branches hiding her from the dog's view. He went over to the rhubarb patch, peed on the leaves. Then he must have decided the coast was clear and started to dig. Tinkerbell sat up and quietly observed the intruder for a long second, then ...

Hisssss! Tinkerbell leaped off the bench and, in three strides, was right by the dog's tail. The dog yelped, jumped a couple feet in the air, and took off down the block — with ten-pound Tinkerbell nipping at his heels.

That dog never crossed into our yard again.

Even though the dog was gone, once Kari and Casey came along, at times, they pestered Tinkerbell to no end, so when she had enough, she escaped outside and scampered up my trunk to hide.

I loved Betty's girls, but Tinkerbell will always be my hero.

***

Bernie kept up Mama Ida's flower garden for a few years, but eventually, she started to slow down and finally decreased the size to about a quarter of what it was. At this stage in her life, Bernie was older than Mama Ida was when she bought me.

It's hard to imagine them the same age as Mama Ida and Papa George. Wasn't it just yesterday they were playing catch and croquet in the yard?

The vegetable garden also got smaller, since she was only using the produce for herself, and most of the berry bushes were pulled out. Even the bridal wreath bush died, infected by some bugs that killed it.

Even though I was jealous of that bush, it seemed to attract the family for pictures at times. I'd welcome any excuse for my family to stop by more.

However, Bernie still had the massive rhubarb patch. Various members of the family stopped by occasionally and cut stalks down for pies and cakes. And, even though Mama Ida's bench began to show some wear and tear, Bernie looked it over each spring and if there was a rotting slat, Dick or Jim stopped by to replace it with a new one. Then she'd come out with a can of paint and gave it a fresh coat. But she didn't seem to have the time to just sit on it and primarily used it to hold a pot or two of geraniums.

Over the next few years, I noticed there was some resistance where my roots were trying to grow. I was now taller than the old two-story house, but, because I had grown so big, it also meant that my roots needed to spread out, and anything in their path eventually gave way. I soon noticed the narrow, uneven sidewalk that looped the house began to push up.

Is that me doing that? Oh, no. I hope Bernie won't get mad.

One day, Bernie came over with a couple of men to check it out. They said, "Well, we could fix the sidewalk, but it's really no use. Your tree here is getting too big and the roots are popping the cement up. It has to come down. Otherwise you're wasting your money."

Bernie looked up at me and said, "It's only a private sidewalk that goes around the house. No one but family uses it anyway. My mom bought the tree years ago, and it's named after her. She means more to me than any sidewalk."

The gentlemen shook their heads as they left, but Bernie looked at me, smiled, and said, "Right, Little Ida? It's only a dumb old sidewalk. What would Mom say if she were here and thought I'd cut you down just because of that?"

Bernie left the sidewalk as it was, pushed up in spots, sunk into the ground in others.

I'm sorry to be so much trouble, Bernie. I guess Kelly was right all those years ago.

***

One day in September of 1971, Gerrie had a meeting in the living room at Bernie's house with all the family.

This looks serious. I hope no one is in trouble, especially me. Since the men told her about the sidewalk, I've been a little worried.

All the sisters came, plus Jan, who was now nineteen years old and a freshman at Lawrence University in town. Betty was last to arrive and, once she got Kari and Casey settled on the floor, playing with their toys, Gerrie got to her feet.

"I'm going to need all your help. You know I've been doing the city treasurer's job on an interim basis since Mr. Feuerstein retired a couple years ago. It's an elected position and he wanted me to see if I liked the job before making the decision to run, plus he said it would give the constituents a better idea of who I am, come election time. This will be the first time a woman has run for this type of position, and if I want to keep my job, I'll need all the help I can get. I've heard there are a few men, including the former mayor, running against me."

Bernie asked, "What can we do to help?"

Gerrie smiled and said, "It would help if Lucy, Pearl, and Betty moved back into the city limits. Living in Grand Chute doesn't help me."

Everyone laughed. "We can still help," Pearl said after the laughter died down.

"Yep. All hands on deck. I'll need to print signs and get them out onto yards, mail pamphlets telling people who I am, and just walk around neighborhoods, knocking on doors."

"I can lick stamps. Mommy taught me where to put them on envelopes," Kari offered.

Gerrie looked amusedly toward her goddaughter. "Yes, you can help. Casey, too." Then she got serious again. "Can I count on all of you to help?"

Everyone either nodded or voiced their agreement.

"What's your platform?" Lucy asked. "All candidates need a platform to run on."

Gerrie thought for a moment. "Well, first off, the people of Appleton are my boss and I intend to have all the tax payments collected with a smile and thank you."

"Oh, that's good," Bernie said.

"Secondly, I plan to keep the staff that's there. They all do a great job, have years of experience. and are very dedicated. Finally, technology is starting to creep into the job and the city needs to be prepared for it. I've gone to some conferences where they said that soon, computers will take the place of handwritten ledgers and adding machines. Some of the big cities are already using them, so I want to make sure the city of Appleton is also."

"No adding machines?" Betty said. "That sounds intriguing. Wonder if it could help me in our plumbing office."

"I doubt that, Betty. These machines would take up quite a bit of your office space. I really think these are designed to help large companies with calculating all their accounts. My insurance company just got the go ahead to build a complete wing onto our building so we can install a huge computer. I'm hoping it will help my department speed up claims," Lucy said.

Betty replied, "Who knows? They just put a man on the moon a couple years ago, maybe they'll make these things small enough to use in every office."

"One can dream, Betty," Lucy said.

Over the next few months, I saw the family knocking on doors in my neighborhood, plus I saw LaBore for City Treasurer yellow and black signs in yards as far as I could see. There were lots of nights Bernie returned late and then got up early to go to teach because she was helping all she could. It paid off. In April 1972, Gerrie became Geraldine LaBore, City Treasurer of Appleton.

Boy, Mama Ida and Papa George would be busting their buttons with pride if they were here. I miss them so much.

CHAPTER FORTY-TWO

There wasn't much activity around the old homestead anymore. All the grandchildren, except for Kari and Casey, were adults and had their own families and lives to keep them away. Bernie continued to take care of Kari and Casey during the summer. I enjoyed those days. The girls found Betty and Bernie's old softball gloves and they played catch in the yard. Once in a while, Bernie brought out the old croquet set, helped them map out a course, and let them play. Of course, they were sisters, so occasionally Bernie needed to referee, but not too often. Even though they were much younger than when I'd originally met their mother, I could tell from how competitive and coordinated they both were that they were going to be as good as she'd been, no matter what sport they played.

One summer, Bernie taught the girls a song that she'd learned while being the Arts and Crafts Director at a summer camp about twenty years ago. I think she regretted teaching them it afterwards, because the entire summer, they broke out in that song seemingly constantly. Even I knew the words by the end of July:

On top of spaghetti all covered with cheese

I lost my poor meatball when somebody sneezed

I can't go any further. My branches shudder every time I think of it. If I never hear that song again, it will be too soon!

***

Bernie also continued to host her rotating turn of Sunday dinners. Even though it was only a few times a year, I got to hear the cards being dealt and the arguing of who played what card. Some things would never change.

***

One Thanksgiving, Bernie was the host. There was an unusually early large snowstorm that hit the area two days before Thanksgiving, so there was lots of snow. After dinner, Kari and Casey came out by me to make a snowman. They rolled up a big ball of snow and had just finished a second smaller one, when Gerrie rounded the corner of the house and joined them.

"Would you like some help?" she asked.

"Sure. How come you're outside and not playing cards?" Kari answered.

"Well, the cards haven't been too kind to me lately and this snow reminded of a Thanksgiving snowstorm that happened when I was a little older than you are. I wanted to see if it was as magical as it was back then."

The girls looked a bit puzzled, but Casey said, "We're trying to build a big snowman and we're too little to put the second ball of snow on top of this big one. Can you help?"

"Don't you think a snowman is a bit boring? Why don't we make something else?" Gerrie asked.

"Like what?" both girls chimed in unison.

"Let me think." Then Gerrie reached down, grabbed a handful of snow, and balled it up in her hand. "Oh, this snow is perfect packing snow. We should be able to build whatever we want."

Casey didn't even hesitate. "Let's build a snow turkey! You know, because it's Thanksgiving!"

"Great idea, Casey. A snow turkey it is. We have the base, now let's see if the three of us can hoist that second ball on top of this big one."

At first they tried to use get the smaller ball on top, but it wasn't working.

Kari said, "You know, if we just add some more snow to this bottom part, we could use our hands to form the turkey."

"You mean dig into the snow to form the features? That's a great idea, Kari," Gerrie replied, already slightly out of breath from trying to get that second snowball on top.

They added more snow, used their hands to carve wings on the side of the larger snowball, then made two smaller snowballs and placed them in front of the large snowball to carve the feet. They built up the top front to form a combined neck and head. Casey went over to the driveway and found a couple of large stones to use as eyes.

What would have all the grandchildren done if they'd ever paved the driveway?

"It's starting to look like a turkey, but it needs a beak," Gerrie said. "Let's grab some more snow."

They each got some snow and tried to attach it to the face but were unsuccessful. They were discussing what they should try next when suddenly the window near me opened. Jan poked her head out the window and said, "There you are, Mom. I thought you were just going to check on the girls, not stay out there with them."

"We're building a snow turkey."

"A snow turkey?" Jan said, and I saw her roll her eyes. "Your sisters want to know if you're coming back to play cards."

"You have to finish helping us make our snow turkey, Aunt Gerrie," Kari pleaded.

"Please?" added Casey.

"You heard them, Jan. I'm staying out here to finish the snow turkey," Gerrie said.

I heard Dick's voice coming from inside. Gerrie was too far away to hear it, but Jan's head turned.

"Jan, what is she doing out there? Is she in or out?" he yelled.

"Keep dealing her out, Dad. She's building a … um … snow turkey," Jan hesitantly answered.

"She's building a what?" I heard him shout.

"A snow turkey. Like a snowman, but in a turkey form." Jan was trying to stop from laughing.

"What the hell is she doing out there? Doesn't she know she's too old to be doing things like that? Tell her to get in here."

Jan couldn't hold back her laughter anymore. "If you want to tell her to come inside because she's too old, you do it. I'm certainly not."

One thing I know about my girls: don't say they can't do something, because they will do it just to prove they can, whether they're eight or eighty.

Jan stuck her head back outside. "I'm cold. Dad said to have a good time playing in the snow." I heard a non-intelligible word come from Dick.

"Hey, Jan, before you go, can you ask your Aunt Bernie where she keeps Grandma's old conical sieve? It will help us make a beak," Gerrie asked.

I saw Jan shake her head, but a few minutes later, she had the sieve in her hand. "Here you go, Mom. Knock on the window if you need anything else."

About another hour later, and after a few initial fails before successfully getting the beak to stay on, a beautiful big snow turkey graced the yard.

I'm sure, even though Gerrie feels like a girl again, her body will tell her a different story tomorrow.

***

Sadly, these family times were few and far between. The only constant activities were the various birds and Peanut's descendants that roamed the yard. Being able to view the neighborhood now wasn't as exciting as it used to be. The kids had grown up and no longer played in their yards or the quiet streets surrounding their houses. The little store located a block away closed and was torn down, so everyone now took cars to get food. No more families walking there to pick up a few things or grab a cold pop when it was warm.

The best part of my day was when Bernie came home from school and needed to cross the yard from the garage to the house. Once in a while, if it was nice, she wandered over by me. She'd stand quietly, staring at me. I think at times, I helped remind her of Mama Ida and Papa George.

I'm lonely. I miss my family. Don't they know how much I miss them? I was excited for them to grow up, but I didn't realize I would hardly see them anymore.

***

Even though I tried hard to direct my roots elsewhere, they kept moving closer and closer to the house. In early fall of 1973, Bernie came over to me, and this time, Dick and Jim were with her.

They turned to Bernie. "We know how much everyone loves Little Ida, but her roots are starting to push at the foundation. If something's not done soon, she'll damage the house," Jim said.

Dick said, "I looked into whether we can move her to where Gerrie and I live, but she's too big now, and she wouldn't live through the move. But this is your house and Little Ida is part of the family, so I know this is a very difficult decision."

After they left, Bernie looked up at me and said, "What are we going to do? This isn't just a dumb sidewalk now. It's the house we all grew up in that's in danger, but I just can't bear cutting you down. Well, I can't think about this right now. I'll make a decision after Christmas. I'm in charge of the school children's church program this year, and I'm so busy with that. Hmm, Christmas. That just gave me an idea." She left me and hurried into the house.

Uh-oh. This doesn't sound good for me. I think Bernie has no choice but to cut me down. I can't stop my roots from spreading out. I am curious why Christmas gave her an idea. Maybe they'll use the top part of me as their Christmas tree this year. Not sure if I like that, but I always did want to go into the house and wear the star. Maybe this is what's meant to be. I sure wish Papa George had listened to Kelly all those years ago, though.

I didn't see her again until she came out several days later to rake the yard. She was humming Christmas carols. When she got near me, she stopped and looked at me sadly. "Oh, Little Ida. I figured out the best solution I could. It's not ideal, but it will have to do."

Whatever is best for you, Bernie, is okay with me.

CHAPTER FORTY-THREE

A few weeks later, the air turned really cold, and the first snow started to fall, all flakey and soft. It was a bright, crisp December day, a couple days before Christmas. I heard a loud noise coming down the road and then I saw a very large truck drive up and park close to me. A few cars that followed behind pulled up, too. Soon, Bernie came outside, along with several men who carried ropes, saws, and burlap.

This looks just like when the farmer came to take me to the pig fair. Only instead of a shovel, they have saws. I know in my heart they've come to cut me down.

I looked around the yard one last time.

Well, if today is my last, God gave me a beautiful day. Even though I won't be able to watch over the girls anymore, they're all settled and happy with life.

The men stayed back while Bernie came up to me. "Little Ida, it breaks our hearts that we have to cut you down. But even though this has to be the end, we would never just let you leave us without a special going away gift. These men are going to carefully cut you down, take you to our church, and decorate you. You're going to be our church's Christmas tree. Now everyone will know how special a tree you are."

A Christmas tree ... I'm finally going to be a Christmas tree. Not just a Christmas tree—the Christmas tree!

I stood tall and straightened out my branches as far as I could. I was ready.

The men, waiting for Bernie to give the okay, looked up and said, "What a beautiful tree. Don't worry, Miss Leinwander. We'll take good care of getting her to the church."

"My father took great pride in keeping her trimmed when she was younger."

Well, at least all those trimming sessions paid off.

The men walked toward me and two of them grabbed each end of the bench, now missing a couple of slats, one in the back and one on the seat. I heard Bernie sigh, then she said, "Let's put it directly into the garage. I'll figure out what I want to do with it later."

She pointed toward the small door that led into the garage, then moved in front of them and opened it. I heard some loud banging and scraping against the concrete inside the garage, but a few minutes later, all three of them emerged and walked back toward me.

Bernie stayed with me the entire time. The men cut my trunk straight, gently lowered me to the ground, and wrapped my branches in burlap so they wouldn't be damaged on the way to church. They were as gentle as possible, but when they cut me from my roots, it did hurt, but not as bad as I thought it would. I looked at Bernie and there were tears in her eyes. I think it hurt her more than me. I vaguely remember how the scratchy burlap felt back when I'd had it wrapped around my roots those many years ago when I was first dug up and brought here.

Once they loaded me onto the back of the truck, Bernie climbed into the cab and occasionally looked out the back window to make sure I was okay.

As we drove to the church, we crossed the same bridge over the large river as when I'd first arrived at the house, anxiously wondering what would happen to me. Once we were on the other side of the river and the truck slowly chugged up the hill, we turned right and drove a few more blocks toward a very large brick building with two tall steeples. The sign said St. Paul Evangelical Lutheran Church.

We're here.

It was a struggle to get me inside. They had both center doors wide open to try to accommodate my girth. I have to admit, it did hurt some when they needed to shove me through the opening, but that part was over quickly.

They hauled me down the main aisle to where several more people, including the rest of Mama Ida's daughters, were waiting to help put me in a stand and decorate me. Bernie joined them, carrying a box.

While I was still on the floor, Bernie came over and fastened a star on the very top of my branches so it wouldn't come loose when they put me upright. Then she whispered, "These people are friends of mine. They're going to take good care of you and decorate you really pretty. Between you and me, I know they don't have enough decorations for you, so I brought some of Mom's favorite ornaments to help out, so she'll be here with you in spirit. And they let me put our family Christmas star on the top of your branches. I have to go now, but I'll be back tomorrow night for the Christmas Eve service."

Oh, Bernie. You have no idea how much I've wanted to wear that star.

I saw boxes and boxes of multicolored glass balls, gold garland, and strings of lights sitting on the front pew, but there were two boxes of ornaments I recognized.

Those are the ones I admired each year. I see the one that's white with gold sparkly stripes around it and the red one with the silver sparkles that has the manger scene on it.

My concentration on the boxes was interrupted by the men using their ropes again to raise me upright and gently place me in the stand. Then they put up ladders next to me, and the women, including the girls, started taking the ornaments out of the boxes and putting hooks on them.

Those ornaments look big. I hope they're not too heavy. I've worn the lights before, but I never had ornaments on.

First, the lights were wrapped around me, followed by the ornaments and garland which were hung on most of my branches.

The ornaments and garland aren't heavy. I barely feel them. I was so worried they were going to bend my branches down. With no roots, I'm glad I won't need to waste my energy on that.

Then they turned on the tree lights to make sure everything was working. At first, no one said anything. Then in the darkness, there was a slow whistle, and someone exclaimed, "Wow. I've been responsible for the church Christmas tree for over fifteen years, and we've never had a tree look so … perfect. The congregation will be so amazed when they see her."

I've never been so proud and humble at the same time. I'm making people happy.

***

Once everyone left, I was able to concentrate on the interior of the church my family loved and talked about so much. It was even more beautiful than I imagined. I was tall, but I didn't even come close to touching the ceiling. I'd been placed up front, beside where the altar was. To my left, there was a beautiful white pulpit that had small statues of the apostles set inside the base. Looking back toward where they'd brought me in, I saw rows and rows of polished wooden pews that only were broken up by a middle aisle, with aisles located on each end. The aisles were covered with bright red carpeting, which also extended to the area where the altar stood. Looking up, I could see a beautifully carved balcony that gently curved the width of the church. On the sides of the building were gorgeous stained glass windows, each depicting a scene from Jesus' life.

The church was all decorated for Christmas. Poinsettias were placed all over the front of the church: on the altar, on flower stands surrounding the altar, on the floor next to the altar, on the steps leading up to the altar, pretty much everywhere it was possible to put one. Attached to the sides of the pews on the main aisle were candle stands filled with candles waiting to get lit. On the side walls, wreaths were hung between each stained glass window, and an evergreen bough was draped from the top of the balcony.

No wonder the family loves coming here. This church is beautiful and I'm making a huge contribution to it this Christmas.

CHAPTER FORTY-FOUR

It's finally Christmas Eve. During the day, more people came and put paper bags under me. I overheard someone say there was candy, popcorn balls, fruit, and nuts in each of the bags, one for every child who came to church that night.

I have presents underneath me, just like a regular Christmas tree.

The organist came in and practiced songs, and others scurried around, making sure everything looked perfect. Later, I could tell through the stained glass windows that it was starting to darken outside. People came in and sat in the pews toward the back. I guess no one wanted to sit close to me. I thought the people who decorated me thought I was really pretty—actually perfect, I remember one person said—but I guess I wasn't as perfect as they thought.

Finally, the church was full—well, except for the first six rows on both sides of the main aisle. Not one person sat there.

In the distance, I noticed Betty, Lucy, Gerrie, Pearl, and their families sitting in the crowded back of the church. I wanted to yell at them, "Hey! There's no one in the front. Why isn't any of my beloved family sitting by me? I'm lonely up here by myself." It took a bit with all the commotion for me to notice that Bernie, Kari, and Casey were missing.

Where are they? I thought Bernie said she was going to be here. She must have the girls and they're running late, but tonight of all nights to be late?

Just then, the lights in the church dimmed and everyone became very quiet. The organ started to play, and the back doors opened. I heard faint singing that grew louder as I saw columns of children stream from the openings and march toward the front of the church. They filled up all the rows by me that were empty.

I'm not going to be up here alone on my special night. The rest of my family must be coming now. I see them. I see them! There's Kari with her classmates, and Casey with hers. Oh, there's Bernie, leading her class down the middle aisle, singing at the top of her lungs.

During the Christmas Eve service, the children sang and recited the Christmas story: all about "a baby which was born this day in the City of David, a Savior which is Christ our Lord." They sang many of the carols I'd heard my family sing over the years.

Toward the end of the service, the lights in the church dimmed again so the candles and the colored bulbs wrapped around my branches were the only sources of light in the whole church. The organ started playing, and I recognized the song instantly: "Silent Night." I'd heard it every year around Christmas time coming from the house.

Before anyone sang, the children stood up and turned around in the pews toward the congregation. Their voices started softly, but then grew stronger. It was the German version my Mama Ida had sung all the time.

"Stille Nacht, Heilige Nacht
Alles schläft; einsam wacht"

Then, I heard more voices, mostly the warble of older ones, as those in the congregation who knew the German version, joined in, with Bernie leading the way.

"Nur das traute hochheilige Paar.
Holder Knabe im lockigen Haar,
Schalf in himmlischer Ruh.
Schalf in himmlischer Ruh."

After the children were done, they turned back around and sat. The organist continued to play the song, with the congregation singing all three verses in English.

I looked down at my family during that song, and tears streamed down all my girls' faces. Even their husbands had tears in their eyes. This was my moment. My time to shine. Everyone in church was looking at me because they all seemed to know the words. I straightened my trunk and stretched my branches up heavenward the best I could. I wanted to make sure my family was proud of me.

Once the service was over, Dick and Jim came up by me and gave all the children the bags of candy that encircled me. When Kari and Casey came up with their classmates to get their bags, they were bragging to all their friends. They said, "This is Little Ida! She's our tree. Isn't she beautiful?"

It took a while, but, finally, everyone left for their family celebrations. Even though I wasn't at home to enjoy the usual Christmas festivities, I was really tired after all the excitement of being cut down, transported, decorated, and finally the church service. I actually was glad when the lights were turned off and I could rest. I realized I wouldn't last much longer, so I needed to conserve all my energy for however long they needed me. But it did give me this time to think and reflect back on my life and how great it was.

***

I proudly stood up front through the holidays: Christmas Day, the next Sunday, New Year's Eve, and New Year's Day. Each day, I felt my branches grow a bit heavier, my energy draining. The ushers and caretakers did their best, but it was the beginning of my end.

I was fine with it, though. Everyone has their time, even trees. Life is about living and dying. I was luckiest because I was able to end my life having the biggest honor a tree like me can have: being a church Christmas tree with my entire family around me.

And now that I've had time to think back on my life, I wouldn't trade a minute.

***

The day after New Year's, my family came to take some remembrance pictures of me when no one else was around. Casey ran up to me with a newspaper in her hand and said, "Look, Little Ida. They put your picture in the newspaper, and in color, too."

They turned on my lights and snapped picture after picture. Even though it was very hard, I did my best to straighten my trunk and stretch out my branches one last time. I wanted them to have the best pictures to remember me by.

As they were about to leave, Kari said to Casey, "It's time to say good-bye to Little Ida."

They both came back down the aisle and touched my branches. "We love you, Little Ida. We'll miss using you for hide-and-seek, playing with your pine cones, and seeing the birds build their nests in your branches." Then, with sadness in their voices and one last touch of my branches, they said, "Bye, Little Ida."

Lucy, Bernie, Gerrie, Pearl, and Betty also came up to me, this time with no tears in their eyes. "None of us will forget you. You were the most beautiful Christmas tree—everyone is saying that. Please let Mom and Dad know we're all doing fine when you see them in heaven."

I sure will. I'm going to miss you all, too. Thank you for giving me the most wonderful life a tree could have.

The lights went out and the door closed. I was too tired to straighten my trunk anymore and my limbs sagged badly. I remembered back to that first Christmas tree I'd seen. How sad it had looked. For some reason, however, I wasn't feeling like that.

Then I heard a familiar voice calling to me ....

"Little Ida, look how pretty you are. I'm so proud of you and what you've become. But I missed you. Papa George has a bench all ready for me to sit next to you again. Welcome home!"

***

All was quiet. The snow fell and another winter had begun.

THE (HUMAN) FAMILY TREE

George "Papa George" Leinwander	1883-1948
Ida "Mama Ida" Leinwander	1885-1959
Lucile "Lucy" Leinwander Schroeder	1913-1998
Clarence "Kelly" Schroeder	1911-2000
Bernice "Bernie" Leinwander	1915-1999
Geraldine "Gerrie" Leinwander LaBore	1917-2004
Richard "Dick" Labore	1912-1985
Pearl Leinwander Gerrits	1919-2001
Leonard "Len" Gerrits	1914-1991
Betty Leinwander Cutler	1923-2008
Jimmie "Jim" Cutler	1926-2015
David "Davey" Schroeder	1939-1921

All was quiet. The snow fell and another winter had begun.

Mama Ida   Little Ida in Church

About the Author

 Karen Cutler Drecktrah has lived in Wisconsin, primarily the Appleton area, for most of her life. As a young child, besides running around all over her neighborhood and their wooded backyard, she was an avid reader. (Thank you, Aunt Bernie for always taking the time to get me to the library). Once, during the children's summer reading program, she reported on 121 books. She's been an athlete for most of her life, focusing a majority of her time on tennis, and winning the Wisconsin Junior College tennis championship in 1982 (the first athletic championship for Wisconsin Lutheran College). She graduated with an Associates of Arts degree from Wisconsin Lutheran College and a Bachelor of Arts in Recreation Management from Carthage College. She currently works as an Accounts Payable and Plant Payroll Accounting Clerk at a local dairy manufacturing company.

She continues to be an avid reader and picked up writing about ten years ago when she discovered her mother's original copy of *Little Ida.* Her mother, Betty, wrote this as a short story for her sisters and family as a Christmas present back in the 1980's. Karen also has had a couple Christmas stories published in anthology books and narrated her story, *The Unexpected Moment of Happiness in the Hospital with my 89-Year-Old Father*, which was about her father, Jim, on the national radio show, *Our American Stories.*

Karen currently lives in Appleton with her husband of over thirty-two years, Bill. This is her first novel.

Follow Karen and Little Ida on:
Facebook: Author Karen Cutler Drecktrah
Website: https://karensmusings371865922.wordpress.com/
Instagram: Authorkarendrecktrah
Twitter: @lobberluv